UNDER HIS PROTECTION

LEONA WHITE

Copyright © 2024 by Leona White

All rights reserved.

No part of this book may be reproduced in any form or by any electronic or mechanical means, including information storage and retrieval systems, without written permission from the author, except for the use of brief quotations in a book review.

❦ Created with Vellum

ALSO BY LEONA WHITE

Mafia Bosses Series

The Irish Arrangement ‖ The Last Vendetta

The Constella Family

Under His Protection

BLURB

A life-altering debt.

A silver fox savior.

A forbidden love that could destroy us both.

At 22, I'm running for my life.

Hunted by a ruthless motorcycle club.

Desperate. Alone. Out of options.

Until *he* claims me.

Dante Constella. 49. Mafia boss. Dangerous desire personified.

My protector. My temptation. My ruin.

Our lifeline? A fake relationship that shatters every boundary.

His power shields me. My innocence disarms his rivals.

It should be simple. Uncomplicated.

It's anything but.

One touch sets my body ablaze.

One kiss promises sinful delights I can't resist.

With each moment, our charade crumbles.

As enemies circle and shadows deepen, fate intervenes:

I'm carrying his child.

Now, it's not just passion at stake—it's survival.

In Dante's world, love is a death sentence.

Can what began as pretense become our salvation?

Or will our forbidden bond be our ultimate downfall?

"Under His Protection" is a scorching age-gap mafia romance featuring a dominant silver fox, a feisty young heroine, and a fake relationship that ignites into an inferno of desire. Brace yourself for lethal family secrets, unexpected pregnancy, and a love that

defies all odds. For mature readers only—this dark, steamy tale will leave you breathless.

1

DANTE

Dante

Romeo sat in a chair, waiting for our meeting to start. He didn't look up as I approached. Instead, he locked his serious gaze on his phone, no doubt obsessing over the details about a business arrangement he would supervise. I gave my only son free rein in the family. The Constella Mafia organization had always been run by the patriarchs of the family, and one day, it would be Romeo's turn to be at the head of it all.

But not yet.

I winced as I finished crossing the patio. "Isn't it too early to look so glum?" I asked, mildly sarcastic as I reached for a chair and pulled it back.

All right. Too much with the weights today.

He smirked, squinting his blue eyes against the brilliant sunshine. As he slid his sunglasses down to cover them, he huffed a laugh. "And aren't you too old to think you can handle that much in the gym?"

I didn't entertain that with a reply. While I wasn't vain, I was proud of taking care of myself, and that included a meticulous fitness regime. That was also why I definitely should've known better than to press that much weight too soon. I'd ignored the rule of thumb about a ten-percent weekly increase, and I would be paying for it. Stretching my arms above my head, I lightly groaned. "You're only as old as you feel."

"And I'm guessing you're feeling over your fifty."

I shot him a look as I relaxed into my chair. "Watch it." Come this fall, I would be fifty, but I didn't dread it. I'd outlived my father, who'd outlived my grandfather. In our world, mortality ran on the skimpy side. We thrived with violence and anted up to any danger. I intended to maintain my position as the Boss for many more years yet. Romeo knew it, too, and that was why I was confident he was merely joking.

And his attempt at humor was welcome. Ever since he'd taken the blame for three of our Constella soldiers being killed, Romeo had been sour and bitter. He struggled to overcome the survivor's guilt, and I hoped he would continue to lighten up and move on from that unfortunate incident. The sooner we all moved on from the Domino war, the better. Dust was still settling from that massive drama within our world, but with every day that passed, things calmed down again.

"Sorry I'm late," Franco said as he hurried across the patio. Behind him, two ornate fountains tinkled and streamed water. To my left, the pool lay sparkling and still, begging for me to jump in and swim. He wasn't tardy to a party, which this lavish outdoor space was designed for, just a small gathering.

"You're not," I told the man. Even though he was a distant cousin, he was still an employee of the organization. Without Franco, Romeo and I would struggle to keep up with running the many businesses of the Constella empire. This rugged bodybuilder was our highest-ranking capo, and I'd never discipline him for being behind schedule. I maintained a busy agenda, but I didn't know how he handled his.

"I had to get rid of the 'guest' again." He rolled his eyes as he sat, emphasizing that word with air quotes.

"Who?" I glanced between my son and my capo.

"Who else?" Romeo muttered, putting his phone in his pocket.

I settled my expectant stare on Franco, who sighed heavily.

"Vanessa Giovanni," he replied reluctantly, as though he didn't want to bother me with her name.

Goddammit. As I looked toward the house, almost expecting the woman to appear, I tried to hold back a cringe. Tried and failed.

"Don't worry. She's gone," Franco assured us.

"This time," I quipped. Vanessa was young and gorgeous. Sexy. Cunning. And completely unwelcome around my home.

"We've had the guards watching out for her car at the gate," Franco said.

Romeo snorted. "Which she's clearly figured out because she comes in a different car every time she *just so happens* to stop by."

I shook my head, zoning out a bit as I watched the water ripple over the rim of a shell carved in the fountain. Years ago, I would've been flattered. My first wife died thirty years ago, and those three decades since had been lonely. Sure, I slept around when I cared to, but I'd lacked any true sense of companionship for far too long. My work—managing and building all the Constella businesses—served as a preoccupation from the fact that I was a bachelor. Vanessa wasn't shy about her interest in me, but she projected it in a predatory manner that turned me off.

"May as well just fuck her and get it over with."

I narrowed my eyes at Romeo. "Hell no. She'd only try to dig her claws in deeper."

Franco removed his sunglasses, fortunate to be seated in the shade. "Do you think she's after *you*? Or the money and name?"

Romeo laughed. "Probably all of the above."

We weren't here to chitchat about how attractive I might be to a woman like Vanessa. She was a bombshell in her own right, and countless men would salivate over a chance with her. As the eldest daughter of the Giovanni family, another Mafia organization, she had her own family wealth and influential name.

Or maybe she doesn't anymore. Franco had a good point. "Just how badly was Stefan hit with the downfall of the Dominos?"

"Financially?"

I nodded.

"I can't give you a number. No one will say for sure, but by my best estimate, he lost quite a bit by allying with the Dominos." Franco glanced at Romeo, who nodded.

"Stefan lost product, men, and a lot of investment money that won't be recouped," Romeo added. "By backing the Domino family, Stefan stood to surrender a lot."

And he had lost, sorely. Just a couple of months ago, the Domino crime family was deep in the throes of war. After they were beaten and taken down, their friends suffered in kind—including Stefan. That was the biggest reason I was cautious about my former friend. Stefan and I were once close, true friends when we were young and stupid. Since his alliance with the now-defunct Dominos, I wasn't sure I could find the will to trust him again.

Franco cleared his throat. "If Stefan is sending his daughter here to con you, though..."

I shook my head. I highly doubted that was the case.

Romeo shook his head as well. "Vanessa was chasing after him even before the Giovannis backed the Dominos."

Vanessa had never been shy about her interest in me. "She's not going to con me." She would just pester me, show up unsolicited and uninvited, and make her infatuation public knowledge. Her desperation wouldn't put her ahead of any other woman who had her sights set on me. What it did was make me extra cautious of ever lowering my guard. It would be nice to find a woman to spend quality time with, but I didn't want the hassle of dealing with Vanessa throughout it. The woman simply didn't understand the meaning of *no*.

"Of course not," Romeo said. "No one's conning us—any of us—ever again."

Franco and I shared a glance at my son's gloomy comment. It seemed that he would take his guilt to the grave. While he had been conned and lied to by the traitor who got our soldiers killed in a fight with the Dominos, the incident was *not* Romeo's fault.

Suggesting that he *let it go* would stir up more emotions, and it was simply too damn early in the day for that. "Especially not Stefan," I said. "I don't trust him since the end of the Domino power in the city."

"He's been acting strange," Franco said, "but I'm not surprised. His association with the Dominos is something everyone will remember for a long while."

Including me. Back when I met and married my wife, as a young man of eighteen, I was friendly with the heir to the Giovanni name. We were two young men—Mafia princes—born with the knowledge that we'd inherit great power.

"Even though you were allies long ago," Franco said, "we'll keep an eye on him. And his daughter."

"We weren't allies back then. We hadn't come into power then to form alliances. We used to just be... friends."

"With Henry Bardot, too," Romeo said, referencing another name from my past. "Who recently passed away, by the way."

I gave him my full focus. "Henry is dead?" He'd gone into the military while Stefan and I took over our family's businesses. It'd been years since I'd seen my best friend, but I assumed he'd stay in the service until his very last breath. "Was he killed in combat overseas?"

Romeo nodded but shook his head and lifted a finger. "Not in combat. I heard that he was discharged and ended up straight in hospice care."

"Heard from who?" Franco asked, always keen to track facts, not gossip.

"Ricky," Romeo answered, mentioning Henry's only son. "I saw him at the gambling halls a couple of months ago and we caught up a little bit. He mentioned Henry having cancer, and I saw that he'd passed."

"Damn." I rubbed my jaw, pensive about this news. Henry was about my age, and this hit hard. He was too damn young to be dead, that was for sure. Living a life in combat had to have aged him, but my life treated me no differently. I was exposed to constant danger and fighting, yet I was still here. "I can't remember the last time we spoke." It had to have been quite a few years ago, during one of his visits home when he came to see his son and daughter. I'd never cared much for Ricky, but I also never stopped him from coming to the gambling rooms above the steakhouse we owned. And his daughter, hell, I hadn't seen her since she was a child. A quiet, bookish sort of girl who seldom said more than hello in passing.

"Hey, that kind of shit happens," Franco said soberly as he held his hands up. "People disappear. They drift apart." He said it like he spoke from experience.

That's the truth, though. All three of us, Henry, Stefan, and I, had once been close. Before our lives and careers changed us, we spent lots of time together. Then Henry went into the military and stayed there. I focused on taking over the Constella organization when my father was killed, and Stefan had always tried to compete, making the wrong choices along the way and hoping our friendship would be a resource for him to fall back on.

"And life's too damn short for that." I furrowed my brow at the gravity of my own words. I was far from being *old*, like my son teased. Even if I was, I'd planned for the future. Romeo was a good son, a Mafia prince who made me proud. One day, it would be him leading the family here. Not me. I never cared to think too deeply about my mortality, but in light of hearing that Henry had passed away, I was forced to think about the future.

It was only Romeo who'd mourn me. I had no other children. No wife. And I disliked the sense of loneliness in those facts. I loathed spending the rest of my life like this—beholden to my work and staying as fit as possible before my body would betray me by slowing down.

"Too short for what?" Franco asked, raising his brows. "Too short to let people see themselves out?" He shrugged. "That's just how it goes."

He always made comments like this, but I couldn't put my finger on who'd done him wrong. Now wasn't the time to figure it out, either.

I sat up and drew in a deep breath. "Is there anything else?" We agreed that life was too short, and I felt that deep in my bones. I'd never turn off this urgency to move and get things done. There was too much to oversee and accomplish within my limited time, too. While I led the Constella organization, I would do all that I could to secure a solid future for Romeo and his children. For all the generations to come after mine.

Our every-other-day meetings were a routine that ensured we were all kept up-to-date about anything of importance. But today's topics worsened my mood. The faint strain in my overworked muscles annoyed me too.

"The Sarround Gala is coming up soon," Franco said as I stood.

I nodded. "Yeah, yeah, yeah." *That stupid-ass party is only good for talking business.*

Romeo got to his feet as well. "I can't say I'm in the mood to party."

I hoped he would be one day soon. He couldn't live in guilt like this. Not for good.

"But Dante, if you don't intend to take Vanessa," Franco said, walking inside with us, "maybe you should secure a date to ward her off."

Now I had to hunt down a date? I didn't have time for that. Waving him off, I dismissed the chance of ever looking for a woman again.

2

NINA

Nina

I tied the knot tighter on my server's apron. Glaring up at my "older" brother, I clenched my teeth and took out my frustration on the length of maroon.

"Ricky," I started.

"No." He shook his head, sending his longish brown hair flopping over his brow again. "Don't use that tone with me, Nina."

I sighed, trying to find some rare, hidden reserves of patience. I had none. "Ricky, don't be a dumbass."

"Stop scolding me," he volleyed back, proving we were world-class bickerers. I bet lots of siblings fought, but none of them had to deal with a moron like my brother.

"I'm not scolding you. I'm *telling* you to go home."

He rolled his eyes and snatched a biscuit off a tray that passed by.

Tessa, my best friend, swatted at his hand. "Don't get caught taking food on the clock."

With a full mouth, he grinned at her. "I'm *not* on the clock. You are."

Tessa and I weren't only friends. We worked together, too. She was the sister I never had, and I could count on her to have my back in educating my brother.

"Yeah." She flicked her finger back and forth to indicate both of us dressed in our Hound and Tea uniforms, ready to spend hours on our feet all night, waitressing at the steakhouse. "*We* are on the clock. Because *we* have jobs."

"And because we have a job and have an iota of financial common sense," I said as I jabbed my finger at his chest, "you should listen to us!"

He groaned.

"Going upstairs to gamble is *not* common sense," Tessa said louder.

We only had so much time on our break back here. I supposed I was "lucky" that Ricky had stopped in here on his way upstairs to the private gambling rooms that were totally illegal. Dad seldom visited, but when he did, it was time for the "boys" to hang out, and they did so up there. I'd never spent a minute on the second floor of my workplace, and I never wanted to.

"It's all about luck, Tessa," Ricky cajoled, like he was such a charming, suave guy. He wasn't.

"No, it's not." I crossed my arms. "You've already burned through *all* the money Dad left us in his will—"

"He left it to me, Sis." He flicked a finger at my brow. "Not you. He left it to me."

I smacked the palm of my hand on his brow, resulting in his wince.

"No. He left it to *us*, but because you're older, you were supposed to divide it between us."

"Well, I'll make it all back." He smiled like the idiot he was, always confident that things would magically just turn around in life. I used to think it was a delusion. A defense mechanism. We were raised by our old, cranky grandmother while our dad was off in the military, and she was horrible with making or keeping money. Our mother ran off after I was born, and Dad cared more about being present for the army than he ever was with us. Ricky and I hadn't grown up with the best background, and I guessed that his inclination to take risks and gamble was a product of that.

"Ricky," Tessa said in an exasperated tone, "you were in debt before your dad passed away. Now you're only in deeper debt, losing everything he left you." She narrowed her eyes at him. "And you *know* half of that was for Nina. What makes you think your so-called luck will improve tonight?"

I covered my face with my hand. "Don't encourage him."

"I'm not. I'm merely pointing out that he's not going to be lucky. Ever!"

He chuckled. "Prepare to eat your words, girls."

I thrust my fists down at my sides. "We won't! It's not a matter of luck. It's about odds. The statistics of it!"

"Like you'd know," he scoffed. "All you do is read and act like a loser homebody." He buffed his nails on the front of his shirt. "Don't worry about it. I got this handled. I got an idea that'll make it all back."

I don't even want to know. "An idea," I deadpanned.

"Yeah." He smiled wider, smug and stupid. "And it's genius."

"You? A genius?" Tessa mocked.

He frowned. "Hey."

"Ricky, do not go up there and gamble another penny." I sidestepped to block him from leaving the cramped small corner of the Hound and Tea's breakroom in the back of the kitchen. Tessa noticed that I was physically trying to deter him from going up the stairs.

"There are other ways to get back on solid ground," she advised.

He hardened his face into a scowl. "Oh, yeah? You speaking from experience?"

I dropped my jaw. "Shut up." That was uncalled for, tossing her circumstances in her face like that.

"What?" Ricky shrugged, feigning innocence. "It's true. She's just as poor as we've ever been—before or after Dad leaving us any money."

I gritted my teeth, wondering how this guy could share any genes with me. He was an imbecile. "It doesn't matter. You can't hold that against her."

Tessa held her hand up to quiet me down. "I don't care. He can say whatever he wants. It doesn't change the fact that I—that we—know what we're talking about. Going up there to gamble is not the answer."

I nodded, grateful for my friend. "Exactly."

Ricky wasn't impressed. "Oh, so we're supposed to do what, then? Wait ten more years for you to waitress to make back a fraction of what I happened to lose?"

"*Happened to lose?*" I fumed, stepping into his personal space and ready to punch him. "Nothing *happened*. It's not some natural disaster that struck. You chose to gamble. You made the decision to throw it all away. Every penny you've touched, you've thrown it away in the name of fucking luck!"

He rolled his eyes, standing up straight. "You don't understand."

"I understand that you are clueless, Ricky. Completely clueless, and you will never learn. You should've let me take over the account once it was cleared."

He was quick to shake his head. "What? No. I'm the man of the family now."

I laughed. It began as a light chuckle, morphed into a harder giggle, and ended as a hysterical cackle. "You've never been the man of the family. You've never tried to keep a job for more than a month, and you squander away everything *I* make while trying to take care of you!"

"Then I'll pay you back tonight," he bit out. "Trust me."

I grunted a dry laugh. "I can't. There is *no* way I can trust you."

Leaning in closer, he towered over me and tried to use his height to intimidate me. "Too bad. You're gonna have to learn how to trust me tonight."

"Ricky, just go home, all right?" Tessa pushed his shoulder to get him out of my face. "Go home, have a beer, and take a nap or something. Just stay out of those gambling rooms."

He reared back and stuck his hands on his hips. "You're never going to get it. Both of you. You're always going to think you can tell *me* what to do. That you're in charge of any decisions around here."

"I should be!" I shouted and didn't care who heard. "I should be in charge of all the decisions about our future."

"Too late," he snapped.

"Nina? Tessa?" our supervisor hollered from further in the kitchen. "Get to work! Your shift started five minutes ago."

Ricky smirked and clapped his hands twice. "Chop, chop, girls. Go work your asses off. Slave away for pathetic change while *I* go and make a fortune." He turned and sauntered away toward the stairs.

I stayed there, glowering at his back until he disappeared.

Tessa sighed and nudged my arm. "Come on. Let's get to it."

"I hate him," I muttered, meaning it yet not.

"Okay, but there's no point in trying to beat common sense into him." She tilted her head for me to go in with her.

She was right. Ricky was a lost cause. Hopeless. All that I could do was secure my tips somewhere he wouldn't find them and use them. The entirety of what Dad left us was gone, and I saw no way any supposedly genius idea of his would bring him out of severe debt and have him come out on top.

All through my shift, I thought of little else. Of how much I loathed my brother, how ironic it was that he was the older one of the two of us and therefore able to impact *my* cut of what was left to me, and how terrible it was of him to help himself to what was owed to me.

Guilt snuck in too. I despised myself for these circumstances because I truly did love him as a sibling. He *was* family, all the family I had left now. When Ricky and I visited Dad at the veteran's hospice, Dad made me promise to look after him, fully aware until his last breath that Ricky wasn't the brightest guy out there.

But how can I look after him when he takes and loses every penny we've had?

"It'll get better," Tessa advised vaguely when we had a moment to clear tables later.

"I don't see how."

"I know how."

I shot her a dubious glance.

"You could find a sugar daddy. Or marry some rich, old dude for money." She smiled widely, teasing.

"I'm not selling myself like that."

She giggled, stacking up plates the busboy was too lazy to get. "Why not?"

"Trade in my independence and dignity to what, suck old, sagging balls for an income?"

Her face scrunched as she laughed harder. "I think you're describing prostitution now."

I shrugged, wishing I could feel lighthearted enough to join in on her laughter. "You should consider it yourself." I arched a brow, watching her grimace.

"To avoid your parents pushing you to marry Elliot."

She mocked a gag. "Please. Don't even mention his name."

Her reaction to that name was always the same. I never understood the semantics of it, but since Tessa was a teenager, it seemed that her parents had gotten it into their heads that Tessa would *have* to marry the son of their friends. "They can't actually expect you to see that through, right?"

Her shoulders lifted and fell in a shrug. "I prefer not to think about it."

I shook my head, tidying up the things to bring back to the dishwasher. "You're talking nonsense, anyway. Marrying a rich old man?" I stuck my tongue out. "No thanks. I can't say that the idea of marriage appeals at all."

Smiling wider, she joined me on the trip to the kitchen. "You got that right. I'm not in a rush to have any man tell me what to do or make decisions for me."

Lucky you don't have a brother like mine, then.

I nodded at her. "Who needs men, huh?"

"Not us," she cheered, infusing as much pep as she could into her voice.

3

DANTE

Dante

Although the Hound and Tea brought in mediocre sales, the building was far too profitable to ever consider closing it. The private, top-secret gambling rooms on the second and third floors of the building raked in significant amounts of money. It also served as a common ground for men to speak freely. Countless business deals were struck in these rooms. I'd personally arranged multiple transactions and agreements across the tables.

I didn't go through the rooms often. Romeo sometimes liked to supervise the happenings there, and tonight, I joined him and Franco. Most of the men were acquaintances of mine anyway, and those who weren't fell under the category of my enemies. They warranted a closer look.

Stefan Giovanni sat in the corner, speaking with a couple of capos, and I wasn't sure how to classify him anymore.

As soon as he caught my attention, he tipped his chin up in acknowledgment.

I fought the urge to curl my lip in annoyance. Instead of turning away, I walked nearer to say hello. If he was intent on becoming my enemy, all the better to keep him close.

"What brings you by?" Stefan asked after we greeted each other.

Other than the fact that this is my fucking establishment? I kept my hands in my pockets, cool and aloof as I shrugged. "No specific reason." *What brings you by?* More to the point, I wanted to know why he was so curious about my actions. Was he trying to keep tabs on me?

"Haven't chatted in a while," he said, almost as indifferently as I had spoken.

"I'm a busy man, Stefan," I replied as I noticed Franco summoning me to come toward him. "Excuse me." I nodded at the men he sat with and left to speak with my capo.

"What was that about?" he asked as I reached him at one of the many small bars. He kept his voice to a whisper, and we both hid our mouths behind our glasses.

"What do you mean?"

He arched a brow. "You looked irritated."

Shit. I'm not hiding my emotions very well. I was a master at disguising my reactions and wearing a blank face. When boredom snuck in, or when I became restless for whatever reason, I tended to slip. "I am. Because if that fucker is here, his daughter will be too."

He sipped his whisky. "Hmm. I thought maybe you'd heard."

"About what?"

"That Giovanni was betting with a cheater." He tilted his head to the side. "Romeo and another floorman caught some idiot cheating."

Cheats were not allowed to last long in here. It had taken me far too long and required too much money to establish one of the premier gambling locations. I wouldn't let fools ruin our reputation.

"I'll deal with him myself," I said, eager for the chance to inflict some pain. Maybe that was all I needed, a chance to vent and release this bottled-up energy I couldn't explain.

"Careful," Franco warned. "I had him pulled aside. He's in the room upstairs."

I nodded. The fourth floor was reserved for holding people—those caught here and elsewhere. In a large organization like the Constella outfit, we needed multiple places to stow people, both dead and alive.

"Why the caution, then?" It was hardly the first time I'd tortured a moron who'd dared to break the rules on my turf.

"He's with the MC."

I clenched my jaw. I was sick and tired of hearing about that motorcycle club. The Devil's Brothers was a stupid name, and the men making up the "organization" seemed even stupider, ruthless and prone to violence, but inferior to the class we maintained among the older crime families. They were trying to be the new kids on the block. So far, they'd done plenty in killing damn near all of the Dominos. But they weren't welcome past that point. And they definitely weren't invited to these gambling rooms—*my* gambling rooms.

"Who let him in?" I demanded.

Franco shook his head. "Romeo's asking the men at the door. It sounds like maybe they slipped in with a disguise, but there's no mistaking the cheat as one of those MC men."

Great. That's just fucking great. If I were to torture one of their men, I would be making a statement against them. Reaper, the club's so-called President, would use anything as an excuse to fight. I didn't fear them, but I sure as shit didn't want the headache of putting up with them directly.

"Thank you." I dipped my chin in acknowledgment and set my empty glass on the bar top.

He snagged my arm before I walked away to say, "If you want backup, just say the word."

I snorted a laugh. This was no laughing matter, though. "This is bullshit. Having to walk around on eggshells and be careful not to piss off the newcomers?" I raised my brows, daring him to argue with me.

"I know what you mean. But with the way they decimated the Domino family…" He shrugged.

"The Constellas have ruled in this city for over a century. Some gang of motorcycle dumbasses isn't going to change that."

I left him with that statement and sought my son. Maybe torturing this cheat would help snap him out of his guiltiness. Violence wasn't always the answer, but for dark bastards like us, sometimes it helped to improve our moods.

Before I could track down Romeo, someone else caught my attention. Vanessa. She strode up to me in a narrow hallway between rooms, and I groaned. The noise was hidden with the music and chatter throughout the floor, but I wouldn't have cared whether she heard me or not. While I didn't want to cause a scene because I loathed drama, I'd told this young woman *no* enough times that it was aggravating to repeat myself.

"My answer hasn't changed," I told her deadpan.

"Dante." She leaned in close to press a kiss on my cheek. "It's so good to see you again." Not stopping there, she worsened her greeting with an awkward, one-sided hug that ended up feeling like a clingy, full-body grab. I resisted a shudder, but I couldn't hide a wince as I extricated myself from her grasp.

"It's been too long since I've had a moment to talk to you." She didn't quit easily. Next, she took my hand. Her fingers were too thin and icy cold, almost like she was an icy mold of a person. With a forceful tug, she attempted to steer me toward another room that was quieter.

"And you don't have a moment now, either." I slid my hand away and stuck it in my pocket, determined to prevent her from grabbing at me again. "I'm busy, Vanessa."

She was either deaf or oblivious. "Oh! I *love* the way you say my name." Plastering herself to me, she wrapped her arms around my neck in a hug. The maneuver pushed her fake tits up against my chest, and with the speed of her reaching out to me like this, I was pushed to stumble backward. I wouldn't encourage her. I would not put my hands on her and accidentally give her a damn ounce of hope. When she smeared her lips over my neck, kissing me and moaning as she ground against me, my impatience snapped. My annoyance shifted into anger.

"Enough." I thrust her away. Once I had her at arm's length, my elbows locked so she wouldn't try to weasel closer, I waited until she looked me in the eye to see how serious I was. "No more, Vanessa."

Her smile remained loose and lopsided, and not for the first time, I figured she was intoxicated. Probably coke or pills since she didn't smell like any booze. I'd witnessed her snorting lines before. It wasn't my business, and I wouldn't make it mine.

"I am not interested."

Still, she grinned like a lunatic. "Of course, you are." She dragged her fingers along the low-cut hem of her dress, enticing me to look at her goods. I'd seen them. She'd flashed me before, at a party, and I wouldn't change my answer.

This woman wasn't just obsessed with fucking me. She was obsessed with just getting her way, and she'd made me her target.

I was sick of her coming on to me so strongly. Really, it was stupid to turn her down. Her breasts were fake, but more than a handful. Her skin was smooth and tight. Her face was young and sultry. She was every man's walking wet dream, but she didn't do anything for me. Maybe if she didn't come on so strongly. If she were anything of a challenge, I might have been curious. I enjoyed the chase and the push and pull of sexual tension. With her, there was none at all.

"I am not interested," I repeated as I released her. My stern echo must have made an impact because she didn't launch herself at me again. Pouting slightly, she stared at me until I turned away.

I resumed my search for Romeo. If anyone should accompany me to torture that cheat, it should've been him. The rooms were all packed, though, and walking from one to another was no easy feat. It didn't help that I was stopped constantly, sometimes just to say hello, other times to ward off deeper discussions I wasn't in the mood to have here or now.

Although the gambling hall was crowded with men and their arm candy, it wasn't elbow-to-elbow just yet. I could slip through well enough, but avoiding Vanessa was another obstacle. She trailed after me, always somehow within sight, and I was tempted to give up altogether.

At this rate, all I wanted was to get the hell out of there. Catching Franco in passing again, I told him as much. "Fuck it. You can deal with the man you took upstairs." He could torture the man who'd dared to cheat here.

"Hey, I was looking for you too. Giovanni's been asking where that MC man is."

I furrowed my brow. "The one who was cheating?"

He nodded.

Interesting. If Stefan was consorting with MC men who cheated... *What does that mean, though?* Was he hurting for money and wanting to make a few quick bucks? Was he so desperate for money that he'd gamble and befriend the enemy who caused him to lose so much in the first place? The whole concept of keeping friends close but enemies closer often rivaled the principle of an enemy of my enemy being a friend of mine. The Devil's Brothers ruined the Domino

Family. And Stefan aligned the Domino family with the funding and support of the Giovanni Family. Now that the bikers ended the Domino rule…

What the fuck are you planning, Stefan?

I turned, seeking out my former friend, and saw Vanessa's smiling face as she approached through the crowd.

Dammit. I ran my hand through my hair, growling in frustration. I was sick of this bullshit. At least I was for tonight. "You handle it," I suggested to Franco. "Because I'm out of here."

He noticed Vanessa beelining for me. After a pat on my shoulder, which coupled with his push for me to go behind him and exit, he sighed. "Go on. I'll keep her from chasing after you. But for fuck's sake, man. Go get laid or something. Let another woman put a claim on you, even temporarily, to make this one back off."

I huffed a dark laugh. "I'm not even sure that would work." I patted his back in reply and hurried to leave.

4

NINA

Nina

At the end of my shift, visions of burning my shoes flitted through my head. These dressy flats were old, with hardly any cushion left to the sole, and I was past due to replace them. With how long I had to be on my feet waitressing at the Hound and Tea, replacing my footwear was a necessity, albeit a necessity that wouldn't be seen to. Not with the shitty lack of money in my life.

When Dad passed away, Ricky and I were both stunned. First, that Dad knew about the cancer but chose to hide it from us. Then, that he wanted to spend the remainder of his viable days of functioning away from us, still serving for as long as he could. We'd been notified too late, *after* his discharge, and saw him only for a little bit of time when he was at the hospice.

I wouldn't lie. I was glad to see him out of pain after all that suffering he'd hidden from us. And when we were told about the amount that would be left to us—which was no great wealth but to us, a bounty—I was thrilled that while he'd been so selfish to never be there as a father, he'd give us something after he was gone.

"But it's not there," I whispered to myself as I finished cleaning the tables in my section and mused about Dad's death. Ricky had seen to the rapid disappearance of all that our father left us, and I wasn't sure I could ever forgive him. If he wanted to lose his half, fine. I would've been responsible with mine.

"Hey, Nina?"

Speak of the devil.

I turned slowly to face my brother as he entered the dining room. The Hound and Tea was now closed, and without any customers in here, my supervisor wouldn't care if he walked through.

"Hey." It was on the tip of my tongue to apologize for how I'd talked to him earlier, but the logical, stubborn part of me wouldn't allow it. He needed the tough love. He had to be told that he couldn't be trusted with money. More than anything else, I deserved every right to tell him how mad I was that he'd lost my half of what Dad left us.

"You about done in here?" he asked.

Tessa had already left. Her dad came and gave her a ride, but she had to leave right then. He wasn't in the mood to wait for her to wrap up her duties. I offered to stay and finish cleaning up her section since I walked home every night—further abuse on my poor, tired feet.

Ricky never came to give me a ride. He was often home playing video games or off doing who knew what. We shared an apartment, but we were more like roommates than family.

Because we always argue about money. Until he changed, it would continue to be a point of fighting. I refused to back down because I was already doing everything I could to avoid our being homeless.

The fact that he was here now, asking if I was finished working, raised alarms. "What do you care?"

"I, uh, I've got a favor to ask you."

I let my head tip back and groaned at the ceiling. *You have got to be kidding me.* "A favor?" I deadpanned as I faced him again. "You want to ask me for a *favor?*"

He winced at how I raised my voice.

"I am not giving you my tips," I warned. Tonight had been busy, likely because the customers ate here and then went upstairs to gamble. I never asked questions about what went on above the Hound and Tea. I learned long ago to simply be grateful for the steady influx of people who'd tip me *before* potentially losing their money up there. Nothing could be overly legal about it, and I adopted an ignorance-is-bliss mentality.

"I don't... I don't need your tips." He lowered his gaze and bit his lip.

Huh? That was a first. I crossed my arms. "You don't need my money?" *Yeah, right.* My brother declining a chance to ask me for money didn't make sense. It implied he had his own money, and that was bullshit.

"Yeah." He cleared his throat, and I tensed up.

Shit. That's two tells now. Ricky was likely a terrible gambler because he was too damn easy to read. First, the lip bite, now the clearing of his throat. He was nervous.

"What's going on?" I knew whatever he'd say next would be bad news.

"You know, uh, how I told you and Tessa that I had an idea?"

I narrowed my eyes. "You said you had a 'genius' idea."

"Well, it sort of... backfired."

Imagine that. I wasn't surprised. Something else filled me. I lowered my arms. They, along with my legs, felt leaden with dread. "What happened?" *Backfired* how, *exactly?*

"I lost..." He ran his hands through his hair and fisted the strands as he stared at me, eyes slitted with fear.

What else is new? I cocked my head to the side. "You lost…?"

"You."

A long moment passed between us. It hung heavily, potent with confusion on my part. He lost me? What did that mean? The best I could guess was that he was experiencing, finally, a moment of reckoning where he learned that I'd had it with him. That I was a teeny fraction of a millimeter from ending all my ties with him, my only family. Was he trying to acknowledge that our sibling bond was severed because of our last argument? That I was finally sick of his bullshit and done with him?

"What does that mean?" I wrung the dishrag in my hands, needing to twist something to let out some steam from the tension brewing within me.

"I lost you." He cleared his throat again. "In… a bet."

My eyes opened so wide that it hurt. Shock punched through me, sending my heart rate racing. I breathed quicker with shallow inhales that didn't help. "You *what?*"

"I thought I could gamble on…" He gestured at me. "You."

I opened and closed my mouth, stunned speechless.

"I'm sorry, Nina."

"No." Shock bled out, replaced with fury. "No. You didn't." I rushed past him, hurrying to run. To sprint. To flee. I didn't want to even look at his face.

"Nina, wait." He followed me out of the dining room, through the kitchen, and out to the area where the stairs led up the back of the building. "Nina!"

I whirled around to face him as he grabbed my wrist. "No!"

His fingers locked tight as he pulled me closer. Alcohol rose from his breath, and I scowled up at him. Drinking on *my* dime. Betting on *my* life. The irony killed me. I shook my head, straining to comprehend how this monster was my brother. My family.

"You can't do that."

"I said I'm sorry."

"Sorry?" I screeched it, so bewildered with what he said that I lagged in a physical reaction to his pulling me up the stairs. "You're *sorry*? You think you can just say you're sorry and that's it?"

"I don't know what else you want me to say," he retorted as I fought to break out of his grip. In the narrow stairwell, I lacked ample room to turn and run. People walked both up and down, causing too much traffic for me to slip away. Even if I had full faculty of mind at the moment, it would've been a challenge to break away from him and actually escape. As it was, I was so rooted in shock that everything flew by as a blur.

"This isn't... This is... No. This kind of shit doesn't happen in real life." In movies, sure. Reality was different. He was ridiculous to think this would pan out as he imagined it would.

"I bet you, Nina. And I lost." He grimaced as though the admission of losing hurt more than the audacity of gambling on me.

"You always lose, Ricky. All the fucking time. But this—" I held the door frame to stop him from pulling me into the second-floor landing. "No. People don't gamble on humans. This isn't going to fly."

He yanked on my arm so hard that my shoulder twisted painfully. My brother was a lanky man, but he possessed some degree of strength over me. He forced me inside, and still locking his fingers around my wrist, he leaned closer to snarl at me.

"It will. This kind of shit *does* happen up here. It's not a fucking casino, Nina. It's private gambling. And the people in here do barter with people."

Oh, fuck. Oh, fuck no. Panic set in, and I shoved at his fingers biting into my arm, straining to pry them off me. "No. No, Ricky. This isn't happening."

"It already did happen! I lost the bet. And now you have to go with…" He glanced over his shoulder. "With them."

I went still, locking up so tight that all the muscles in my body ached at once. "With them?" I narrowed my eyes, not even wanting to know. "With *who*?"

He broke eye contact again, and that only pushed me closer to throwing up. It had to be someone bad, someone really bad if he was this uneasy.

"With… the president."

I narrowed my eyes. "What?"

"The president. Of the club."

I stared at him, waiting for his words to click. "Of this gambling club?"

"No. The Constellas own this place."

The faint reminder of one of Dad's old friends did nothing to reassure me.

"The Devil's Brothers," he clarified. "That club."

I gasped, unable to hide my utter shock. "The *motorcycle* club?" I knew of them. I recognized the patches sewn on their leather cuts. I saw them drive their bikes by. All of them were raggedy meatheads, overly muscled and angry looking. "You lost me in a bet to someone in the goddamn MC?"

"Not just someone." He looked back over his shoulder. "To their president. Their leader—Reaper."

My rage hit a high and spilled over. Anger coursed through me, charging me with rabid energy to strike out. I punched, slapped, and kicked. Without conscious thought, I gave it my all to beat him. "You lost me in a bet with someone named *Reaper*? Are you insane?"

In any other circumstances, I would've rolled my eyes at the idea of my brother thinking he could bet on me. Like a human was a thing to possess and barter. That I could be owned and handed over in a transaction of debt. To normal, ordinary, and law-abiding people, it would've sounded ludicrous.

But a motorcycle club? An MC who was rumored to traffic women and children, not to mention drugs and guns and who knew what else?

This was real. Ricky's "genius" idea wasn't a joke, but a tangible, actual debt to uphold.

Fighting him off didn't hurt him, but in my instant reaction to attack him, to strike at him for the sheer stupidity of what he attempted, I earned my freedom. He was too slow to block a kick to his shin, and as he doubled over and crouched from that impact, he loosened his grip on my wrist.

The second his fingers released me, I took off, into the gambling hall, through the hallways, and around corners. Running through the throngs of people, I tried to hide and get away from Ricky the best I could, but there were so many damn people in here. Every one of them contributed to this creeping claustrophobia that dizzied me.

They chatted and laughed. Drank and gambled. Some of the older servers from the Hound and Tea were doubling up here as waitresses hoisting trays of food and booze.

I slowed, unsure of where to go among all these richly decorated and fancy rooms of wealth and elitism. In the corner of another hallway, I spotted two grungier men and instantly identified them as my new owners. Men from the Devil's Brothers MC. They didn't wear their cuts, but they were recognizable, regardless. I knew it when they held up their phones and glanced back at me, as though they were checking the sight of me with an image on their screens.

"That's her," one said to the other.

His friend nodded, and they both pursued me.

"Fuck," I whispered. "No."

I turned and ran, but I didn't get far. Slamming into a rock-hard body was a hell of a way to stop my stride. Firm fingers wrapped around my upper arms, but these hands weren't gruff and possessive. This strong man merely caught me from the collision, preventing me from careening toward the floor.

Scents of sandalwood and cedar wafted from him as I lifted my face from his suited chest. While my heart hammered away, I dragged my gaze up to peer at this tall man who'd caught me. His hold on my arms wasn't tight. He wasn't trapping me here in place, but with the MC guys rushing toward me, I felt like I was stuck and vulnerable no matter which way I ran or where I stood.

"Are you all right?"

Oh, God. He had one of those gravelly, raspy baritones, so deep and low and full of command. I swallowed, trying to understand why his voice seemed so familiar. As I looked up into the ruggedly handsome face of Dante Constella, I knew why.

It'd been years since I'd seen him. Many years. Even though he looked older, I recognized him with a confusing and instant hit of comforting familiarity.

"Nina?" He narrowed his brown eyes. Surprise and disbelief showed on his lean face. "Nina Bardot?"

I nodded, immediately defensive. "You didn't come to my dad's funeral." It was the lamest, stupidest fact to cling to, but it was the most recent detail that pierced through the panic claiming me.

He blinked, not wounded and owning up to my excuse of a greeting. "I didn't. I'm sorry that I was away for business and only heard about his death earlier today."

It hardly mattered now. Nothing mattered. A sense of doom seeped through me, almost rooting me to the spot. Nothing would matter in my life anymore. Not this unbelievably sexy man smoothing his thumbs over my arms, almost like an unconscious afterthought he had no control over. Not the shock of seeing this face from the past again, and like this, here. Not the disrespect of him not attending the funeral of one of his old friends, either.

All I could focus on was the time that slipped away. My freedom would end as soon as those MC men caught up to me. My idiot brother had signed me away to heathen bikers. And there was not a single damn thing I could do about it.

Dante gazed down at me, seeming to overcome his shock at encountering me. He swiped the tip of his tongue over the seam of his lips and furrowed his brow. "Nina?"

I jolted, blinking numbly as I took in all the rugged features on his handsome face. "Hmm?"

"I hope you're not too busy," he said.

I couldn't help the incredulous laugh at that joke. *Busy running from my life, maybe.*

Ever so slightly, he urged me to step closer to his warm body, so fine in that tailored suit. "Would you like to get out of here and catch up?"

I locked onto the promise in his words. *Get out of here.* That was all I wanted. In a trance, cautious in thinking his sudden appearance was too good to be true when my life was coming apart, I nodded. "Yes."

I had to escape. I needed to get away from those bikers until I could figure out a logical step in stopping this disaster of an arrangement from happening.

He lowered his hands from my arms, and I boldly hurried to hold one before I'd lose him in the crowds.

As he glanced down at my fingers linking with his, I swallowed and tried not to sound like I was begging. "Yes, please. I'd love to catch up."

5

DANTE

Dante

*C*atch up?

Talking was the last thing on my mind.

Something about the intensity of her grip on my hand bothered me. She wasn't clinging—all right, she *was*. But it wasn't with the same cloying impatience that Vanessa showed me.

I seldom welcomed women to come on to me. I preferred the chase. The challenge. All the ups and downs of suspense and working for what I wanted to better enjoy the spoils and rewards.

Henry's daughter clutched my hand desperately, boldly, but with a degree of determination that brokered on fear.

Before I led her through the room, I scanned my surroundings. Giving up on looking for Romeo, I noticed Franco dealing with some men. Then other capos in charge. All was well here. Franco could handle that MC idiot who was cheating.

As the boss, I could come and go as I pleased, and right now, I wanted to get the hell out of here with Nina.

"Let's go," I told her, firming my hand around hers. She was dainty, small, and delicate, but I felt the rawness of worn skin on her fingertips.

She didn't reply, and as I guided her through the room, towing her with me, she offered up no sign of resistance to how speedily I ushered her away.

Catch up?

With her hand in mine, I was electrified with a strange, instant zing of lust. If the mere sensation of this minimal contact, her hand in mine, could wake me up like this, I imagined a fuller, more bare touch of her against me would be even better.

Catching up with her was a lie. I'd never really known her before. I congratulated Henry and his ex, Alison, when Nina was born. A couple of times when Henry was home between tours, we visited and I had passing glances of the quiet, bookish girl Nina was then.

I didn't know her. Not back then as she grew up. And I wouldn't assume to know a single damn thing about her now other than recognizing her as Henry's daughter. Reconciling the girl I barely remembered with the exquisite young woman she was now... I couldn't. It was impossible.

"This way," I offered when she seemed to hustle right behind me.

It hadn't left my notice that she was eagerly agreeable to this sham of "catching up". I doubted she recalled anything about me, other than the fact that her father once knew me, yet here she was, ready to go along with leaving with me.

"Where—" She cleared her shaky voice, and I was immediately on edge with how uneasy she sounded. "Where are we going?"

Her common sense prevailed, but perhaps too late. We were already outside, striding toward my car.

I shrugged. "Want to cruise around for a while?"

She lifted her face toward mine. Illuminated in the streetlamps behind the Hound and Tea building, she was cast in shadows and faint golden light. And fucking gorgeous. I caught the wariness in her eyes, and I didn't know how to interpret it. She was willing to escape those crowded rooms with me, but she had her guard up.

Is she mad that I didn't go to her father's funeral?

That was the only recent thing she could possibly hold against me. We didn't know each other. We'd known *of* each other, indirectly.

And I wanted to change that in the worst way as I slowed near my car.

I wanted to familiarize myself with every decadent inch of her sexy body. Every curve. All the smooth, soft skin of her generous tits, her tiny waist. I stared at her lips, fighting the urge to taste them and bite them for the reward of her gasp. And her hair, that thick, glossy braid. I resisted the need to grip it and hold her in place as I shoved my cock into her mouth and—

She cleared her throat, narrowing her eyes with suspicion. The sound jarred me from staring, and I chastised myself for showing how badly I lusted for her.

Watching her raise her brows as we paused at the passenger door, staring each other down in a silently brewing tension, I reached over to grip the handle for her.

"After—"

The door to the building clanged open behind us, and as a group of rowdy men all tried to exit the narrow space at once, I rolled my eyes. Franco and the security guards sure had their hands full tonight. It looked like more of those Devil's Brothers idiots, and I wondered if it was past time to give them a warning to fuck off around here. On my turf.

Nina wasn't as distracted. While I turned to look at the door, she slipped away and opened the door for herself. Her fingers closed over mine as she wrenched on the handle. In the next moment, her body eased away, prohibiting me from enjoying the warm, slender curve of the small of her back, where I'd put my other hand.

She was in the car, already tugging the door closed by the time I looked back at the men exiting the building.

Huh.

I wasn't imagining it. Nina was a little frosty with me, not letting me be the gentleman and open the door for her. It was no matter for now, though. She was in my car, and as I rounded it to get in the driver's side, I considered the sheer stupidity of asking her to spend any time with me.

I lusted for her. From the second she'd bumped into me, a deep, carnal need filled me. But this was Henry's daughter. My best friend's kid. This wasn't right, no matter how much Henry and I had drifted over the years.

But I got in the car, anyway, not wasting a second to speed off with her riding shotgun. In the limited space of the car, her scent overpowered me. Something clean but sweet, and mixed with the scent of *her*, altogether intoxicating. I'd been around countless attractive women before, but something about Nina captured me.

"Interesting running into you there, of all places," she quipped.

"How so?" I arched a brow at her as I pulled into a lot near the gambling rooms. I wasn't sure where to take her. The only thing that crossed my mind was bringing her home and fucking her hard, but that wouldn't solve anything other than scratching a stubborn itch, this quick-to-form and strong desire for her.

"I just learned tonight that the Constellas owned that building."

I set the car in park, eyeing her uniform. "*I* own it."

She turned to look me over. "So, you're my boss. That's the business that kept you so busy that you couldn't stop by at my dad's funeral?"

Rubbing my jaw, I considered whether she was playing dumb or she was really that ignorant. "Henry and I used to be best friends back in the day."

She snorted. "Before he gave up staying in touch with everyone, you mean."

"We drifted apart," I agreed.

"That's no excuse not to come to his funeral."

I kept my stern gaze on her. "It's not." If she was trying to pick a fight with me, it wouldn't go far on this topic. I did feel bad that I hadn't gone to Henry's funeral. "I feel bad that I wasn't informed."

She rolled her eyes, sassy yet not childlike with that juvenile gesture. "Too busy owning the Hound and Tea. I got it."

"Do you?" I asked. Before she could reply, I gave up on resisting her allure. In the privacy of the parked car, smelling her sweetness and wishing I could lean over and touch her, I was weak. Too weak for my liking. I didn't allow women to have power over me, ever, so I got out and walked around the car to open her door. She joined me, standing outside the car and enjoying the quiet and fresh air of this empty lot.

"Do you get it?" I studied her. "We're not strangers—"

"How are we not strangers? I haven't seen you since Romeo and Ricky shared a birthday party."

I did the math. Thinking back to the one time my son shared birthday celebrations with Henry's son, her brother, I calculated that almost twenty years had passed since the memory she referenced. Their birthdays were close together, and we combined efforts to celebrate the boys that one time. *Eighteen years.* It felt like too long ago. But I exhaled in relief that Nina wasn't the jailbait she looked like. She was twenty-two now, fully grown into her womanly figure.

"But Henry knew what kind of businesses I oversaw." I let the silence linger between us, prompting her to agree or argue that point. She merely pursed her lips and looked away.

"I've preferred to lean on the principle of ignorance is bliss." Lifting her face to smirk at me, she added, "And it's not like I've run into you over the years."

I nodded. "Interesting that we'd crossed paths tonight though."

Her brow furrowed. "I wasn't up there to work."

It was news to me that she worked in the restaurant down below, too. "I have my hands in many businesses, Nina. I didn't know you were an employee in the steakhouse."

She shrugged, dismissing that detail. "Not like I'll be going back now."

I stepped closer, confident that my first hunch was right. When she slammed into me and then jumped at the chance to get out of there, I wondered if she was trying to hide. Hell, I was too. I'd been eager to get away from Vanessa and Stefan. Now, with Nina's bitter quip, I wanted to know why she sounded so upset.

"What's wrong?" When she opened her mouth, I cut her off. "And don't tell me you're upset about my absence at Henry's funeral." I doubted that was it. Something else was up, and I demanded to know what.

"I—" She clamped her lips shut and shook her head. As she crossed her arms, I advanced toward her. The hell with that defensive bullshit.

"I asked you a question."

I took her hand and lowered it, physically altering her stance as I urged her to backtrack toward the car. She leaned against the closed door and stared up at me. Only a fraction of fear shone in her eyes, and I hated how her lower lip trembled.

"My brother…" She hesitated, licking her lip and lowering her gaze. "Ricky lost me in a bet."

"He *what?*" I'd never cared for Henry's spineless, dull-witted son.

"Ricky was in debt and he thought he had a 'genius' idea to bet on *me*, like I'm some kind of possession to—" She inhaled a quick breath. Her eyes opened wide as someone neared the lot. By the sounds of the throaty engines, it had to be bikers.

Furious that Ricky would do something so stupid and dangerous at the worst place, at my gambling rooms where illegal deals were struck, I waited for her to finish. "To?"

Her hand lifted toward me. She grabbed the lapel of my jacket, but she had yet to look away from whatever captured her attention behind me. "He lost me in a bet to someone in that motorcycle club. Someone named Reaper." Her throat tensed as she swallowed, fisting her fingers as she curled them around my jacket.

Fuck. You fucking dumbass. Ricky would answer for this bullshit. I had my answers. I knew why she wanted to run from there now.

An idea struck, and even though it was rash, nothing could stop me from wanting to step in and help her.

"Play along," I ordered.

"What?" Lines formed on her brow as she frowned up at me. "What do you mean?"

"Play along." I didn't wait. Those engines could only mean that the MC men had followed and were coming for her.

Too bad for them. They wouldn't get near her now.

But I did. With a possessive hunger I couldn't understand, I stepped closer until she was caged against the car. Sandwiched between me and the hard surface, she gazed up at me and opened her mouth to argue. To demand an explanation. To ask what I wanted her to play along with.

Ignoring her reaction, I lowered my hands to her hips. Flipping up her skirt, I pushed against her.

I had her pinned, panty-covered core rubbing against my growing erection as I wedged her legs apart.

I had her silenced as I leaned in more.

I quieted her protests—all laced with utter confusion—and kissed her hard.

6

NINA

Nina

Dante lunged against me so quickly that I had no time to react. He vaguely instructed me to play along with whatever plans he had, then before I could shove him back and insist on some personal space, he held me up against his car.

His solid body pressed into mine, shoving me back roughly before I could protest.

He hadn't given me a chance to catch up, to insist that he back off. But now with his hard presence firmly locking me in his embrace, I had no willpower or desire to tell him off.

I wanted no space between us. As I looped my arms around his shoulders, hugging his neck as he plundered my mouth, I wanted *no* barriers or distance between us. With his muscled body flush to mine, his hulking size blocking me from the view of those bikers who'd pulled into the lot, I couldn't think of anywhere else I'd rather be, anywhere else that would make me feel this secure.

And wanted.

I inhaled through my nose, caught off guard with how suddenly he'd crushed his lips to mine. One second, I was battling through the humiliation of admitting to this successful and rich man that my brother had stooped so low as to lose me in a bet to a criminal. The next, he was thrusting his velvety and demanding tongue into my mouth and making me both gasp and moan.

I grunted, unable to form words, and he pulled back, out of breath and staring at me with urgency. "Play along," he ordered again before he dove back in and kissed me harder. His hot lips brushed back and forth as he sought a deeper angle. Then his tongue slid inside to steal my taste, exploring without patience.

With need. Hell, the idea of this guy *wanting* me… It was crazy, nonsense, but I did as he told me to. Getting over the shock of his actions, I surrendered to his impulsive idea and tried to play along. I kissed him back. I threaded my fingers up into his thick back hair as I held on to his neck. And I arched my back to promise this kiss wouldn't end, not even for air.

"Act like you want it," he growled, misinterpreting my fidgeting as an attempt to squirm free.

Escaping *him* was the last thing on my mind. Even if those bikers weren't parking nearby and talking loudly, I wouldn't have dared to cease this shocking kiss.

Dante ground against me, forcing me to hook my legs wider apart and higher. It didn't seem to be enough for him. He lowered his arms to cup my ass cheeks.

"Make them think twice about interrupting," he whispered into my ear before he trailed his wet, hot lips along my neck.

The second his fingers slipped under the elastic of my panties, I cried out. Those hard, callused fingertips stroked so damn close to my pussy, and I couldn't help but thrust my hips toward him.

"Yeah, like that. Show them who's got you," he urged, every word dark and filthy with gritty seduction.

I whimpered as he dipped his fingers into the juices he caused to leak from me. I was slick, slippery, and too warm with arousal as he sucked at my neck. Alternating between kissing and biting, then licking away the sting, he ground against me and eased his fingers into my wetness.

As soon as he curled his fingers, moving higher to find my clit, I let my mouth hang open as I groaned.

"Fuck, Nina. Just like that. Let me hear it." He sucked on my earlobe as he rubbed circles around my needy bud. "Louder."

I didn't hold back. I couldn't. Common sense was gone. I wasn't capable of replying, much less thinking. All I could do was hold on as he slid his fingers back to my entrance, grinding his body against mine for much-needed friction.

With the first touch of his kiss, he'd lit me on fire. A sweet, addicting tension built within me, harder and faster, until I was panting with the rush to just come.

"Dante!"

He pushed me to burst apart. One quick thrust of his fingers deep inside me did the trick. His thumb unerringly rubbing around my clit pushed me further. Waves upon waves of relief fled my body, and as I shook and trembled through the bliss that burned so bright, I clung to him. My arms went weak, heavy with fatigue as I kept them draped over his shoulders. Quivering and clumsy, my thighs remained cinched around his waist.

My pulse slowed. My breath came easier. All while he kissed along my jawline, tender, more deliberate presses of his wicked mouth. I leaned against him, limp and drugged with an orgasm I couldn't have counted on.

In the distance, the roar of the bikes faded. They'd driven off, and belatedly, past the fog of desire, I realized what he'd done. What his game was.

He'd wanted me to play along with this little show of... of...

I shoved at his shoulder, getting his attention. "What the hell was that?" Still, I struggled to catch my breath. The way he grinned, looking at my wet, parted lips, filled me with a dose of smugness that I had no right to feel.

"I was showing them that you were otherwise preoccupied." He squeezed my ass, guiding me to lower my legs until I shakily stood between him and his car. Once I was on my feet, he moved his hands lower to fix his pants and zip back up. I'd been so blinded and surprised that I hadn't registered him unzipping and letting his pants hang lower.

From the bikers' perspective and the shadows blanketing this lot between tall buildings, it probably looked like Dante was fucking me against the car.

"You..." I lowered my gaze, taking in the prominent bulge of his erection tenting his pants. He hadn't lowered his boxers. He didn't *actually* fuck me, but he sure had given them a show.

I raised my hands to cover my face. It wasn't shame making my cheeks burn. Not only shame, at least. But I was out of my comfort zone, still acclimating to how quickly this had happened.

Playing along. Pretending to be fucked against the car. But also... coming so hard and quickly like that.

"Why..." I exhaled hard, staring up at him. "Why did you—"

He groaned, leaning in closer to lose his grin against my mouth. With this kiss, he hedged replying, but I couldn't care. I fisted the front of his shirt, blown away by how much I wanted him, *still* wanted him, despite just coming.

"To get them to leave you alone," he replied.

Oh, and the erection in your pants is nothing but a side effect of your heroism? I wasn't sure if I was more upset that he wouldn't admit he wanted me just as badly or that he'd done something so stupid and rash like that. While I'd never take it back, I'd never regret coming like that, I was quicker to consider the ramifications of what just happened.

"They drove away, didn't they?" he taunted as he stepped back and ran his hand over his face, frustrated but triumphant, too.

"For now," I agreed. "Are you trying to get me killed?"

He shook his head.

"You will!" I swatted at his shoulder as I shoved my skirt back down. My panties were ripped from his hand forced under them. They were useless and wet, hanging loose against my thigh. "You'll get me killed after they report back to their leader that another man was touching *his* woman."

Narrowing his eyes, he stepped closer, forcing me to crane my neck to look up at him in order to maintain direct eye contact. "But you're not his woman."

"No, but—"

"But what?"

"I'm not *yours*, either."

His smile was slow and sinister. "Let's say you are. They wouldn't know that you're already taken. They wouldn't have known that before Ricky lost you in a bet."

Anger filled me with that reminder. That my idiot brother dared to bet on my life. Confusion came next. I couldn't make sense of what Dante was suggesting. "I wasn't... I'm not taken."

Setting one hand on the car's roof, he slanted closer. It wasn't close enough for me to feel trapped and safe under his touch, but I was locked in place under his direct attention. "They wouldn't mess with me, Nina. Those biker dumb fucks know who I am in this city. They won't mess with me or my woman."

I set my teeth on my lower lip. "But I'm not…"

He tugged my lip free, staring at his thumb on my flesh. That smoldering gaze taunted me, and I fought the instinct to suck his digit into my mouth. Dante did something to me, making me react without thought and listening to this need thrumming through my body.

Still, the truth remained clear.

I cleared my throat. "I'm not your woman."

"Pretend that you are." He dared me with a serious stare. "Play along."

I blinked quickly, trying to rationalize his offer. "Dante…" I shook my head. "I appreciate your saving me tonight, but they'll be back and—"

"Pretend to be my girlfriend, Nina."

Searching his face, I waited for a tell of his humor. He had to be teasing. Joking. Because a man like him would *not* need to fake this sort of thing. He could have any woman he wanted. Handsome, rich, fit, and… dammit, he was the kind of sexy beast of a man anyone would lust for.

"I wish I could, but…" I looked down, confused over what could work as a counter here. I had no fight in me. The sound of being Dante's woman—even just in pretense—was too tempting to reject.

"But what?"

"But it's dumb." I frowned, facing him again. "It wouldn't work."

"Of course, it would."

I admired his confidence. He probably had many reasons to own it. He also seemed too rash, almost impatient for me to agree.

"Why would you want to protect me?"

He sighed, standing straight and putting distance between us. "I have my reasons."

"Because you knew my father?"

He grunted. "I can't imagine Henry would approve of this." He flicked his finger between us.

A hit of shame warmed me. No, I doubted Dad would like knowing his former best friend had his mouth and hands on me.

"Why would you want to do this?"

"I have my reasons." He adopted that bossy authority again, smoothing down his jacket and lifting his head higher. He oozed dominance and control, and I figured that he expected me to not ask about his reasoning.

I supposed it didn't matter.

"What do you say?" he asked as he picked up my hand and raised it. Studying the red marks left on my wrist, courtesy of Ricky trying to manhandle me, Dante clenched his jaw.

I had no clue what to say. Hours ago, Tessa and had I joked about this very situation, finding a sugar daddy or having a man to protect us from the bullshit of life. We'd both laughed it off, so cocky that we'd always be better off without men in our lives, but now...

Why not? Dante was exactly the kind of strong man who could be my hero—even if we were only pretending.

He arched one brow at me, something I was quickly recognizing as his way of silently demanding an answer.

My heart raced. My mind felt empty and sluggish. Deep down in my heart, I operated independently of this adrenaline rush or the lingering aftermath of an intense orgasm rendering me limp and lazy, sated.

Why the hell not?

I nodded.

"Yeah?" A grin lifted his lips.

"Yeah. I'll… um. Let's do this." I raked my teeth over my lower lip, unsure whether I could manage playing along like *this*. "You and me. I'll pretend to be your girlfriend."

But not for real, right?

He lifted my hand, staring straight at me as he kissed my knuckles. "You and me," he agreed.

I swallowed, worried I was already in too deep.

7

DANTE

Dante

This time, when I opened the door for Nina, she didn't fight me on it. Her gaze remained distracted as she entered the car. After I closed the door, I drew in a deep breath and second-guessed myself.

The idea to pretend that Nina was with me was an impulsive one. I didn't think it through. I operated on impulse, and that wasn't always a bad thing.

It's not like it wasn't on my mind already. Since we'd crossed paths, I battled a persistent need for her. Imagining her naked and bouncing on my cock, I fought the urge to take her as I wanted. Hearing her crying out in pleasure would forever taunt me, and it was the best I could hope for at the moment.

I rounded the car, gritting my teeth. Frustration set in before I reached my door.

I hadn't been thinking when I acted on my lust for her. Sure, it helped her out in the end, but now that we were committed to pretending we were together, I'd ensured endless torture for myself. I wanted her—all of her—but I'd foiled that from being a possibility in telling her that we'd fake it.

I'd made this a business transaction of sorts. I'd keep the bikers away from her, and she'd keep Vanessa off my back. I couldn't trust Vanessa because she represented a tie to Stefan, and having Nina close by would buy me time to get to the root of why I didn't trust anyone in the Giovanni family anymore.

"Tell me exactly what happened tonight," I said as I got into the car. I had no intention of backing out of my impromptu suggestion to fake date this gorgeous, quiet woman, and I planned to make sure it would go smoothly according to how I saw fit.

"With Ricky?"

I nodded, driving out of the lot. She detailed the circumstances that Henry had left them in, and I hated the sorrow that she'd gotten the short end of the stick with the man who should've been her father. A real parent. Nina and Ricky were raised by a grandmother, and their mother was never in the picture. I thought long ago that Alison left because she knew back then that all Henry cared about was his military career.

"Some families are like that," I told Nina. "Devoted to service."

She huffed. "Devoted? Or obsessed?"

I couldn't argue with her there. Henry came from a long line of military-minded servicemen, and I supposed it was a hard habit to break or amend.

"You have lots of men working in your 'organization'. They're probably devoted and dedicated to their jobs."

"They are." Every Constella soldier could be counted on.

"But they also have families, right? Friends and family?"

"We're all one family." It likely wouldn't make sense to her, but that was how it was.

"Well, I'm not sure I have any family left. Not after Ricky did that to me. He took all the money Dad left. Gambled it away."

I frowned as I drove on. "At the Hound and Tea rooms?"

She shrugged. "I don't know. Probably other places, too. So, he lost it all and tonight, he said he had an idea. That ended up being betting on *me*, and losing—of course—and expecting me to go to that biker guy."

I caught a glimpse of her shivering as she turned to look out the window, and I resisted the urge to take her hand. Now that I'd drawn the line in the sand, declaring us as two players in a grand scheme of pretending to be together, I had to keep it strictly professional.

This was how I erred with every deal I struck. Everyone knew their part. Everyone had their goals outlined. No room for confusion. It was why I didn't trust Stefan any longer. Since siding with the Dominos, his goals and the spectrum of where his loyalty lay were no longer clear to me.

"Did he say how much he was betting for?"

Pivoting slowly, she hit me with a laser of a glare. "Are you asking me what my price is?"

I didn't flinch, unbothered by her haughty tone. In fact, I respected it. She had enough sense not to put a price tag on herself—on any person. However, in my world, with other crime leaders as my peers, I knew otherwise. Everything, and everyone, had a worth. And it could always be quantified with dollar signs.

"Did he tell you?"

"No." She resumed glaring out the window, but her fight deflated quickly. Her shoulders slumped. Sinking back into the cushion, she sighed deeply. "I don't even want to know, anyway."

"What did he tell you?" I had to know the details and cover my bases. It entered my mind that I could just offer to pay off Reaper. I could give the motherfucker the number he wanted from Ricky. It could be a payback to Henry, post-mortem, for missing his funeral.

Then again, I wouldn't dare. The second I entered any kind of negotiation or transaction with those biker idiots, it would be become a deeper level of business, and I refused to do *any* business with them.

"I was just finishing my shift at the steakhouse. He showed up and told me that he 'lost' me in a bet to Reaper, and then he tried to drag me upstairs. As soon as I figured out that he meant it, that those people really thought I was a possession, I hit him and got loose."

"That's what the marks on your wrist are from?"

She nodded, rubbing the spot. "It's not that bad."

Stopped at a red light, I turned to face her. "Anyone marking your skin is bad," I growled.

Except... me. I glanced at the redness from where I'd sucked on her pulse point, licking the tantalizing sweetness from her flesh there. Fuck, I really liked my mark on her.

But no more. If we were going to fake this, then I had to keep my need in check.

"Then I saw those bikers, and they came after me. That's when I turned around and ran into you. And then..." She lifted her hand to gesture wordlessly at what followed.

And then I wanted a taste of you and found a way to make it happen.

I sighed. *So much for keeping my life simple.* On the rest of the drive to the Constella estate, a little bit further from the city but not too far, I spoke with Franco. He answered on the first ring, unlike Romeo. He didn't pick up at all.

"I want you to have someone follow Ricky Bardot," I told him. In my peripheral vision, I noticed Nina jerking to face me, her brow furrowed.

"Henry's son?" he asked.

"Yes."

"For...?"

"Just to follow him." It was all the clarification I wanted to give him while Nina could hear. Half of my plans included beating some sense into the young man. He had no business trying to bet on his sister's life, and with Reaper, of all people. More than my need to punish him for his stupidity, though, I had to make sure the bikers didn't retaliate or push the guy to make it easier for them.

My altruism only went so far. Yes, I wanted to save Nina from this situation, but my desire for her fueled that decision. My own interests did as well. As long as she was with me, Vanessa would back the fuck off.

Franco and I talked a little further about having someone track Ricky. He brought up the presence of the motorcycle club members at the gambling rooms, and I debated banning them altogether. That move would also be taken as an "attack" against them, and I wasn't sure if I wanted to mess with them officially like that. Not yet, at least. I saw what happened the last time an MC got involved with a Mafia family—the Dominos were done. Gone. Dead, and broken up as an organization. While I knew the Constella name wouldn't fall so easily, I would do all I could to steer clear of large issues and unnecessary threats.

"Romeo left an hour ago," Franco said as I pulled up to the estate. He wasn't expected to keep tabs on my son. I didn't micromanage him, either. Romeo was his own man and he'd never let me down. I doubted he ever would. However, Franco and I were both more than aware of how poorly Romeo was getting over his guilt in not saving the three soldiers in that fight. It was a testament to how much we all mattered. Like I told Nina, we *were* one big family here.

I wasn't sure if that meant Romeo would be *here*. We mostly lived together, but he had several other properties he liked to stay in as well.

It looked like it would just be me and Nina, though. After I hung up, I got out and rounded the car to open her door.

"What's going on?" she asked, taking in the enormity of my home.

"You're staying here."

"With you?" She gawked at me as I tilted my head in a mute order for her to follow me to the door. Already, a man was approaching to drive the car to the garages, and she was waylaid with watching the man do his duties without order.

"Yes, with me."

Nina hurried to catch up with me, grabbing my forearm. She clutched me to stop me, but I rolled with it, tugging her closer and forming her hand to rest on my arm, with mine over hers.

"You expect me to just move in with you?" she spluttered. "Just like that?" She snapped her fingers, and I stopped in the middle of the steps rising to the front door.

"I do expect you to move in with me. Just like that. Because if you go to wherever you call home, your brother or the bikers will take you. Just like that." I added a snap of my fingers to both mock her and emphasize my point.

She blanched.

"I don't trust Ricky," I said as I led her toward the door. "I don't trust that MC, either."

"Okay. I realize that, but—"

"But nothing," I replied, secretly loving how she would protest and stand up for herself every inch of the way. Pushovers were boring. Obedient, docile, and meek people grated on my nerves. Nina didn't argue for the sake of bickering, but because she wanted to make her voice heard.

I also loved squashing whatever retort she wanted to fling at me. Satisfaction curled within me, warm and potent, and I reveled in the thrill of this push and pull. Per the texts and emails that had come in while I was kissing Nina and fingering her tight cunt, I had many other things to do. But here I was, bringing her into my home.

"Keeping you close is in my best interests."

Her eyebrows dipped as she thought over my words.

Shit. I didn't have the time or patience to explain why pretending to be with her was beneficial for me. "Your staying here, close to me, is in *our* best interests."

"To dissuade the bikers from thinking I would be their leader's."

I nodded. And to give Vanessa the impression I wasn't available, since the times I told her no didn't stick.

"In order to make it believable," I said as I released her in the foyer. She didn't seem to be listening, spinning slowly as she took in the opulent entrance. Her plump lips parted in awe as she roved her appreciative gaze over the stained-glass windows and huge chandelier sparkling and glittering with the low lights from the walls.

"In order to make it believable…" she prompted. She was listening, and I had a hunch she always was. Nina didn't make much of an impact on me when she was a girl because she was quiet and bookish, keeping to herself. But I'd be stupid to assume she lacked any sense of perception and awareness of her surroundings.

Observant. I liked that.

"In order to make this deal between us believable," I repeated, "you will really need to act the part."

She sobered, stopping her survey of the foyer. "Which entails what, exactly?"

When she bit her lower lip, I held in a growl. Was she hoping it might include more intimacy? More chances to fuck? The heavy lidded expression she couldn't hide hinted at it.

"Act the part by living in my house," I said, pulling my phone out since it buzzed in my pocket again.

Nodding, she accepted that. "Okay. It's probably safest, too. I wouldn't trust Ricky if I went home."

"And you'll need to be seen with me, too."

"All right."

I couldn't ignore how quickly and readily she agreed to that point. If she was hoping for a repeat of what we did at the car, she'd be disappointed. Now that we'd entered a deal, we *both* had to stick to what our roles were. The second we blurred the lines, it'd likely fall apart.

"However."

She rolled her eyes. "There's always a catch."

"Don't give me that sass."

She arched her brows. "I won't so long as you don't try to give me any bullshit."

"However," I said again, "I am a busy man."

"I think you've mentioned that." She crossed her arms. Even though her Hound and Tea uniform was simple, her gesture pushed her breasts up in that white blouse. I struggled not to look.

"I am a busy man and I cannot stop my work commitments for you." It was the biggest reason I declined any suggestions to date. It was also why I avoided investing the time to find a woman to be with. Work—all my businesses and deals—had kept me company for thirty years, and changing that was easier said than done.

Nina shrugged. "Okay?"

"I won't be here to pamper you and coddle you."

She smirked. "Was I asking you to?"

That fire. She had no clue how sexy she was like this. "I don't want you to get it into your head that I'm available."

"And why should you be?" She pointed between us. "We're pretending it all. As far as I'm concerned, you're just a roommate here."

Oh, is that so? On one hand, I was pleased that she got it, that she understood I wasn't here to play house with her. On the other hand, though, I wondered how easy it would be to go for it all.

A butler appeared to my side, ready to assist with Nina. He had to have noticed her and assumed she was a guest, not our newest inhabitant.

"George," I said to him while I kept my focus on Nina. "Please see Ms. Bardot to the guest room near my suite."

He nodded.

"See to it that her needs are met for the evening."

"Yes, sir. I will fetch any garments and necessities that she requires."

"But in the morning, please let my niece know that her assistance is required to further welcome Ms. Bardot into our home."

Nina frowned. "Your niece?"

I nodded, though I wasn't certain they'd ever met. "Yes, Eva will help you settle in."

She opened and closed her mouth, glancing to the side. "Uh. Um, Right."

Was she already losing sight of my explanation that I was too busy to play house with her? Or was she merely disappointed that I had to cast her aside so soon?

It's for the better, Nina. I dipped my chin once, as a farewell, before I turned. "Good night, Ms. Bardot," I said over my shoulder.

"You know, calling me by my name would make it more believable," she teased.

"Believable to whom?" I turned slowly, holding my arms out to show that it was just me, her, and my butler. I didn't need to worry about fooling him. He worked for me.

Technically, she does too. I added that to my list of tasks to do—ceasing her employment while she performed this act with me. It wouldn't be safe for her to be near the gambling rooms with the bikers trying to find her. Or her idiot brother.

She got the point, though. Here, in the privacy of my home, there was no need to pretend anything. After a wince, she nodded. "Got it. Good night, then, Mr. Constella."

Fuck me. I wanted to hear her say *my* name again, like she'd cried it out when I made her come.

Clenching my teeth, I ignored my desire and walked away.

8

NINA

Nina

"What's your name?" I asked the butler as he led me up the stairs.

"George, Ms. Bardot."

I studied his profile, amused that he'd stick to such formality. I wasn't anyone to impress. As a working-class woman, I related more with him than the man I was supposed to be "dating".

"Just call me Nina," I told him, shaking my head at how surreal my life was becoming. In the span of hours, my existence had been shaken up and distorted so much that I didn't know which way was up.

First, the audacity of Ricky betting on me—and losing. Then, the fear that Reaper and his bikers would come to capture me. Running into Dante was a strange occurrence, but the way he told me to "play along" as he kissed me and fingered me…

I moved my hand to the other arm and pinched slightly. Pain stung at the point.

Yep. This is real. I'm actually here, *fake dating* him.

It wasn't a dream. Or in light of the bet Ricky lost, it was not a nightmare any longer, either. Dante had shown up at just the right moment and offered me an easy out. Like a hero in the books I liked to read, he'd suggested a solution to spare me from going to an awful gang of bikers.

Instead of trying to accept that my life had really changed this quickly in so many ways in such a short time, I zoned out and took in my surroundings. I felt out of place and dirty as George led me up the grand staircase. It seemed like I was touring a museum with all the fine artwork hung on the tall walls. And as I turned toward a pair of ornately decorated and carved double doors, I braced myself for the rest of this experience of being a fish out of water, of thinking the old story of a pauper and a prince could be reality.

The massive bedroom suite George guided me to enter was fit for royalty. For a princess. Someone with power and importance.

I stood there, gobsmacked, as I scanned the details. Creamy pink walls with crown molding that would be a bitch to dust and clean. Two chandeliers twinkling with subdued light. Like a sea of plush comforters and pillows, the bed waited for me to mess it up. Even the carpet was immaculate, so soft and smooth, looking brand-new to the degree that I worried my junky, falling-apart shoes would stain it.

"I…" I shook my head, slowly snapping myself out of this stupor. "I can't stay here."

George frowned. "Mr. Constella specified your guest room to be the nearest to his private quarters."

I blinked, frowning at this perfect, luxurious place. "I heard that, but… No. I can't." I shook my head again.

"Is there something not to your liking? I can call the housekeeper and—"

I lifted my hand to stop him from pulling his phone out from his pocket any further. "No! No. Don't bother anyone." *Not on* my *account*.

"Ms. Bardot—"

"Nina. Please." I swallowed past the lump of emotions clogging my throat. "Please don't treat me like I'm some sort of star guest or important figure." I added a light chuckle. "It's making this all the more... weird."

He nodded, rocking back onto the soles of his feet. "I see."

I scrunched my face. "Do you?" I wasn't sure if butlers were allowed to share opinions. I wanted his, though. Could this older man recognize how out of place I was here? How utterly different I was and that I couldn't belong here, in this room or as Dante's fake anything?

"I can arrange for you to have another room." He raised his brows.

"No, please. No trouble." I sighed and glanced around the room again, worried I'd break something or dirty a surface. "This is fine."

He nodded, and I could have sworn he smiled slightly. "I'll have Maura bring some clothing options in for you."

"Oh." I hadn't even thought that far ahead, what I could wear tonight. I didn't have pajamas. I had nothing but the uniform I'd had no chance to change out of since my shift ended. Thinking about clothes or personal belongings seemed so frivolous in this context. Figuring out how to adjust to moving in here to pretend to be Dante's girlfriend was enough of a monkey wrench in my life.

How would I get my things? And how long would I even be here? Dante and I hadn't put a time limit on this farce, but with his little warning that he was a busy businessman who wouldn't be here to keep me company, I figured my presence would expire sooner than later.

And what am I even going to do?

Questions pinged in my head, too quick to answer, and all of them accumulating so fast.

Would I still go to work? I had to. How would I make a living? Did he plan to pay me to stay here and hide as his girlfriend? No, that didn't sound right, either. He said we'd need to be seen together, out of this monstrosity of a palatial home.

All at once, I was struck with all the ways I hadn't thought a single thing through. I was the conservative one when it came to risks. I never took them, opting for the safe and easy route through life and staying off the radar. Yet, I hadn't put any sense of planning into telling Dante that I'd pretend to be his girlfriend. Details had to be smoothed out. Agreements and conditions had to be discussed and negotiated. We hadn't talked about *anything*, and I felt stupid not to pay attention and be a smart, logical person about any of this.

I'm only human. I'd been running on fumes after my long shift, tired and spent. Then with the fear of being taken by the bikers, I'd shifted to the fuel of adrenaline to power me through the night. Once Dante kissed me and made me come, though…

I huffed out an exasperated breath and ran my fingers through the remnants of my unraveling braid.

The soft click of the door behind me was the only signal that I was now alone to let these facts sink into my brain. Not wanting to appear dumb or unthankful, I spun to see a panel of polished wood.

"Thanks," I said anyway, too late for George to hear. I bet he wasn't supposed to talk with the guests, anyway, being the hired help and all.

I looked at the bed, then glanced at the door open to a view of a fancy bathroom. Torn with the need to press a button for a do-over of the night, I wondered if I should give my weary brain a rest by slumping onto the mattress and passing out or if I should clean off the grime from work.

Walking through the huge bathroom, I considered how different this was from what I was used to. A shower stall separate from a wide claw-foot tub. So much lighting and ample, fluffy towels. Everything gleaming bright and clean, spotless and new. I felt like a speck of dirt in a state-of-the-art showroom.

So lost in my thoughts and awe about my lodgings, I jumped when a soft knock sounded on the door to my room.

"Sorry to interrupt, Ms. Bardot."

I hurried out to catch a housekeeper setting a small stack of clothes down. "Nina," I corrected.

She dipped her body lower. A curtsy. She freaking *curtsied* to me. I huffed a laugh and tried to wrap my head around it all.

"Please let me know if you should need anything else for the evening." She stepped back as I lifted the corner of the folded pajama set atop a stack of similar soft garments. Pajama sets, nightgowns, even lingerie.

"Oh, this is too much," I protested.

She backed up another step, lifting her hand in argument. "Oh, not at all. We have everything you need in this house." With a sweet smile, she reached for the door. "Should you need anything, just use the landline and choose the button for housekeeping."

I gawked at her, nodding dumbly as she backed out of the room—executing another curtsy—then left me standing there bewildered. The stack of clothing she'd just dropped off likely cost more than two months of tips—good tips.

My fingers felt too grimy to pick up the options and check them out. *I felt too dirty after a long night of work.* "Shower first," I muttered to myself.

It would take a solid night of rest for me to properly sleep on all of this. Dante's rescue. His extreme generosity. This enormous shift to the world of the rich, even if I was only pretending to belong in it.

As I showered, I tried not to freak out about how Cinderella-ish this was of me. It was simply too much to think about, too much to stew on. Once I cleaned up and dressed in a nightgown, I dropped into bed and drifted to sleep.

Dreaming of bikers roaring after me should've had me waking in the morning with restlessness, but surprisingly, I slept well.

I sat up, yawning, and wondered what the hell would happen next. It would take me a while yet to adjust, but I understood the basics. I was here to pretend to be Dante's. It wasn't safe for me to go home at the risk of seeing Ricky or the bikers. And Dante likely wouldn't be here to help me settle in.

But someone else will be.

Curious if and when I would meet Eva, I got up and changed into the casual loungewear that Maura had left with the pajama selections from last night.

No sooner than I dressed and brushed my teeth and hair had someone knocked on the door.

"Yes?" I winced as I went to open it. Should I reply? Just open it? I wasn't sure of the protocol. I was a guest, yet not?

I opened the doors to see a slender brunette. She stared at me, deadpan and unimpressed, and flicked her long, shiny locks of chestnut over her shoulder. Wearing a form fitting dress, she looked on point. Makeup professionally applied. Hair expertly styled. Skin flawless and glowing. And her dress and shoes were straight off a model—with a model's figure to boot.

"You're Nina?" she asked.

While she didn't say it with too much snark, I caught a hint of her annoyance.

"Yes." At least I didn't have to correct her for calling me the stuffy and formal *Ms. Bardot*. "And you must be Eva?"

"Why *must* I be?" she retorted, walking into the room. This woman couldn't be much older than me, but she moved with a sophisticated confidence and maturity, almost like she knew she would be in charge and counted on that never changing.

"Because... Dante said you'd help me settle in here."

She narrowed her eyes and crossed her arms as she looked me up and down. "Settle in, huh? Do you actually intend to stay here?"

Uh... no? I wasn't sure if I should say that, though. *Did he tell her that we were fake dating? Do I tell her?* Again, I lamented the few details I'd hashed out with him about our agreement.

"Because I can't see you lasting long."

Great. Just great. His niece had to have the mentality of my enemies in school. The mean girl. She was the queen of them, that was for sure.

"Why not?" I challenged.

She huffed, looking me up and down. I wasn't wearing my uniform or crappy shoes. I'd showered and tamed my hair. I didn't have much makeup to rely on, but I preferred the fresh-faced look, anyway. I wasn't sure how she could see anything lacking in me on the surface, but I supposed for someone like her, she'd be able to detect when she was in the presence of someone inferior in class.

"You're not his type." She stalked closer, slowly and with a clear warning in her stern gaze. "And if you think you can get your way with my uncle and manipulate him at all, think again."

"Whoa." I held up my hands with my sarcastic reply. "Easy, tiger."

"When it comes to my uncle—and my cousin—I will never go easy on anyone barging in here and being an imposter trying to look like they belong."

She was uncannily accurate with that assessment, and it perturbed me. How could I *look* so different for her to target me as an outsider?

Was it in my posture? The way I spoke or held my head up? I had no clue. For the next several hours, though, as she gave me a tour of the place and then ordered me a wardrobe, I was granted further examples of how I wouldn't ever belong here.

The lavish décor. The top-line items in every room of the house. And all the expensive, designer clothes coming for me soon. Eva, with her icy tone, was right. Nothing suited me here. Nothing made this feel like a home. I *was* an imposter. As the day dragged on with her securing the essentials for me, I wished that I could catch even the slightest glimpse of Dante. Just to have a visual reminder of why I was doing this, of how this mattered.

I saw nothing of him. It was only me and Eva as she ordered so many things I gave up trying to calculate the gluttonous spending. I couldn't justify it. Sure, I couldn't go home, but maybe George or another soldier could go there and pick up some things for me?

I would have felt more comfortable with something familiar. Once Eva left me in the evening, I grabbed my phone and contacted Tessa. I needed her comfort now more than ever.

She answered quickly, worried about the news that I had "quit" at the steakhouse. Even though we didn't want anyone to know that we were pretending to date, I told Tessa the truth. She wouldn't tell anyone, and I needed at least one independent source to know of my whereabouts and why I was here.

"So, that's what I was doing," I summarized. "I wasn't at home getting ready for another shift of waitressing tonight. I was *here*, at his place, tolerating his icy bitch of a niece as she tried to make me look presentable and show me where to go in this mansion."

"She's that bad, huh?"

I felt awful to complain about Eva. I'd only just met her. I didn't *know* her to judge her. Likewise, she didn't know a damn thing about me, but she was clearly judgmental.

"I think she's very protective of Dante and her cousin." I rolled over on the bed, lounging on my stomach instead of my back. As I traced vague circles and shapes on the top of the comforter, I sighed. "And I can't fault her for that. You know, family is family."

Tessa snorted a laugh. "Yeah, right. Don't look at me for votes of confidence about a family. It's kind of wild, though, that you worked for Dante and didn't even know it!"

I shrugged. "I guess it can be a small world, after all." I hadn't told her that he made me come last night. The finer notes about how he'd asked me to play along with him could be something between me and him, not anyone else. I admitted that he'd kissed me, and that seemed to be enough to convince her of this plan.

"And you say he's not bad on the eyes?" she teased of my summary a few moments earlier.

"Not bad?" I groaned. "My God, girl. He's so fine." Slapping my hand over my face, I tried to contain the wide, giddy smile that spread across my lips. "Something has to be seriously, morbidly wrong with me."

She laughed along, sounding so far away on speakerphone. "Why would you think that?"

Aside from the sheer lunacy of entering a fake relationship just to get out of a forced handover to lawless bikers?

"Lusting after an older man?" I huffed a weak laugh. "He's *so* much older than me."

"Age is just a number. This only means that he'll know what he's doing." She giggled. "In every way."

Oh, he does. I didn't want to wonder how many women he'd practiced on to be able to so quickly and effortlessly finger me and make me come so hard like that. I merely appreciated that he could and that he'd chosen to show me. "He's…"

"He's what?" Tessa asked, excitement clear in her tone.

He was so much I couldn't sum it up easily. Generous, giving, cocky, and strong. Powerful and sexy, and so very masculine. "He's very smart." It felt like a cop-out and a compliment at the same time. He was intelligent *and* had expertise in pleasuring women.

"And hot?"

"Oh, fuck, Tessa. *Definitely* hot. I can't stop thinking about…" The urge was so strong to come clean and tell her that he got me off. Yet, I stalled, biting my lip and holding back on this confession. I wanted to keep the memory of him to myself.

"About what?" she urged, still laughing. "Don't keep me in suspense."

"Him." I couldn't bring myself to tell her the whole truth. At moments, flashbacks of his kisses and touches lit me on fire and renewed that instant desire he'd stoked in me. I wouldn't tell her that, though. I greeted her and explained that I was pretending to date Dante to avoid that bet Ricky had made. It'd taken several long minutes to calm her down from the anger about that news, but still, I couldn't outright lie to her. She was my best friend. Best friends were privy to scandalous ideas like pretending to be a Mafia lord's girlfriend. While I knew she wouldn't blab about what Dante and I were doing, I felt sheepish to admit that we'd kissed and that he'd taken the play-acting so far as to actually get me off.

I sighed. "I can't stop thinking about him."

"Well, that's sappy," she joked. "You've got it bad for him, huh? Even though it's just pretend?"

I sighed, wishing I could properly explain how much Dante revved up my desire.

At the sound of a throat clearing behind me, I flinched and dropped my phone to the bed. I spun, finding Dante standing at the doors. I hadn't closed the one all the way, it seemed, because I hadn't heard the hardware click while being opened.

He leaned against the doorframe, arms crossed, his hip slanted against the wall. His bemused eyes were trained on me. At the first hint of a smile or smirk on his lips, I knew he'd heard it all.

"Uh…" I fumbled with my phone. "Gotta go." I disconnected the call and hated how furiously my cheeks heated. To say I was embarrassed would have been the understatement of the year.

He'd caught me talking about him as though I were some foolish, lovestruck woman so far removed from his level of maturity.

"Have a productive day?" he asked, interested but more so, amused.

"Yes. Eva was a tremendous help." *Shit. How long was he standing there?* I hoped he didn't hear me complaining about his niece.

"I'm glad to hear it."

I mentally groaned. *What* else *did you hear just now?*

"Good night, Ms. Bardot." With one dip of his chin, a half nod, he turned and left me cringing and blushing in the throes of humiliation.

"Night," I called out weakly, wondering how I'd face him again after that.

9

DANTE

Dante

Nina and I had to keep our plans secret. That was a given. However, hearing her tell this friend of hers that we were pretending to date didn't fill me with alarm.

Even though I lacked much familiarity with the woman, I felt confident that she was a loyal person, someone who wouldn't betray confidentiality with an enemy.

If she wanted to tell her close friend about what we were doing, I could allow it. She had to have some kind of a story to tell her coworker and friend to explain her sudden absence and hiding.

As soon as I strode off from Nina's room, I fought hard to dismiss the sultry look in her eyes when she spoke about how attractive she found me. I'd watched—and heard—it all. Her badmouthing Eva, which sounded about right. My niece could be icy. About the plans to pretend we were dating. And then sheepish opinions about lusting after me, a man her father's age. Her father's former friend. All the while, she'd relaxed on the bed, stomach down, slender legs kicking in the air and taunting me to stare at her ass. The mirror across the room provided me a glimpse of her reflection as she had her girl talk, and I relished the excited happiness when she talked about wanting me.

She wasn't lying.

Nina desired me.

I felt it, and I felt smug to hear her admit it to someone else.

But I had to resist. We'd only just begun this farce, and I couldn't dive all the way in and confuse it all with fucking her like I wanted to. Sleeping with her would make it all too real. Sliding into her pussy or mouth would make this less of an act and more of a reality.

"Not now," I growled to myself as I headed toward my quarters. I couldn't tell myself to give up on the idea of ever having Nina like I wanted to, but it was far too soon. We had to cement the fact that we were together, first.

In the privacy of my room, I pulled my phone out and looked into the woman Nina called. The call was picked up with the house's tech surveillance, and I easily followed the path to a young coworker named Tessa West. She didn't seem like anyone who'd stir up trouble, and I filed away the information for later.

I wouldn't begrudge Nina for talking to her friend. So long as she did her part here, I couldn't complain. And for the next few days, she did.

Busy with calls, meetings, and discussions with Romeo and Franco, I had little time to even see Nina. I knew she was at the house. She'd taken my order to move in and stay here without any pushback. But I didn't see her at all. That didn't mean she wasn't on my mind. She was. Rooted deeply with a sneaking dose of intrigue, Nina claimed my thoughts in my free time, but I didn't *have* many opportunities to daydream about her.

It felt ridiculous to miss her when she was within reach, right here in my house. It was another example of how I lacked the time or focus to develop a *real* relationship. My priorities were in keeping the Constella businesses running smoothly and ensuring our enemies weren't taking advantage or trying to attack. Those two general objectives had required my attention for so long, I struggled to break out of that habit.

I had to now, though. After stepping out of my office, I headed in the direction of Nina's guest room, more excited about the prospect of seeing her and having a reason to talk to her than I likely should have.

I knocked, and after her reply to enter, I stepped into her room. She leaned back on a chair, legs draped over the armrest.

"Busy?" I asked, sarcastic yet not.

"No?" She closed the book and raised her brows.

I couldn't help but get suspicious that she was being slightly sassy about my approaching her and asking if she was preoccupied after I'd so clearly warned her that I wouldn't be available often.

"I would like your company at dinner tonight."

Placing the book on a side table, she swiveled to face me fully, her bare feet on the carpet. "Oh?"

I nodded. "We'll leave in a couple of hours to meet with some of my business acquaintances at Escott's."

Her mouth parted as she set her vulnerable blue gaze on me. "Escott's. Wow."

Mentioning one of the city's finest restaurants impressed her. Or maybe that was intimidation she was trying to mask.

"You haven't wanted my company at dinner all week."

Has it really been that long already? It felt like just yesterday that she'd come here. Telling myself to ignore all thoughts of her was skewing my sense of time.

"I would like you present so they can see I have a woman in my life."

The slight smirk on her lips shouldn't have been so sexy. "What?" God, she pushed my buttons.

"Well, I would argue that you *don't* have a woman in your life."

I stared at her, marveling in her tenacity not to back down. "Because we're only pretending?" It didn't seem like I was. I envisioned pushing her back on that chair as I knelt in front of her, her sweet cunt as my goal. That image felt so very real, tangible to the point that my dick woke up.

"All you seem to want is your work in your life." She shrugged and stood. "I'm just saying it might be hard to convince anyone otherwise."

"Please be ready to accompany me to Escott's in a couple of hours," I repeated, ignoring her push for a reply.

She couldn't hide her discomfort this time. It seemed that I'd forced her out of her comfort zone with how she winced and blushed.

"Wait. I, uh, I won't be ready." She bit her lower lip. "I don't… I don't have anything to wear. I mean, generally, yeah, but for Escott's?"

"Then we'll stop on the way and get you something." I turned before she could taunt me with that innocent look any further. When she got timid and quiet—shy, even—it turned me on. She was so damn young, youthful and naïve, and it riled me up to want to both dirty her up and protect her, to shelter her.

When I held the door open for her an hour later, I was stuck on a call with a soldier reporting in. Then again, when we arrived at the boutique for her to find a dress suitable for the posh restaurant we'd be going to, I was on the phone with Franco.

Even though Nina and I were together in the car, then at the dress store, I was pulled away with my priorities. I paused in my conversations long enough to direct the store attendant to help Nina find something suitable for Escott's, and then stepped outside to continue speaking.

Romeo chimed in with a three-way call this time, and I wasn't happy with what they had to share.

"All I'll say is that the Giovannis need cash," Franco said. "They've lost a lot, and some of the men under my supervision have been reporting that Stefan is saying he's good for his money because his 'friends' will come through."

Romeo huffed. "And he referenced us? Directly?"

In the corner where his video showed, Franco nodded. "He did. Stefan's been trying to set up new deals, particularly with the movement of guns, but no one wants to work with him after how he'd sided with the Dominos. He's been telling others that the Constellas would vouch for him."

I growled and rubbed a hand over my face. "The fuck he can."

"I lost all faith in Stefan when he sided with the Dominos and backed them up," Romeo said.

He stole the words right out of my mouth. "And I don't trust him one bit now," I added.

"They've lost a lot," Franco said. "It's not surprising that Stefan's desperate for something solid as a backup."

I shook my head. "He needs to look elsewhere."

"He's not even looking," Romeo said. "He's going around and just assuming that he can count on us to stand with him."

"He can't." Annoyance burned hotter within me. "He can't presume that I give a shit about him now. Just because we were good friends long ago doesn't mean that holds true now."

Franco sighed. "This puts Vanessa in a new perspective too. She's been so forward and making it known that she wants you…"

I clenched my jaw. "Which started when it looked like the Dominos would be finished, and Stefan would lose alongside them."

"This is bullshit," Romeo seethed.

I hated the idea of anyone else seeing me as Stefan's ally. It was a false notion, and I had to stop the spread of that nonsense sooner than later. *Starting with this dinner.* I bet some of the men at Escott's would've heard about Stefan's lies by now, and it would be an excellent place to correct them and set them straight.

"I will not align with the Giovannis." I looked at both of their images on the video call, making sure they heard this as directly and firmly as possible. "Not with Stefan. Not with Vanessa."

They agreed and disconnected after confirming that they'd make sure to convey that to everyone else.

Charged with impatience to get to this dinner and do damage control for Stefan talking about something that wouldn't happen, this fantasy of my friendship and vouching for him, I entered the shop and strode toward the fitting rooms.

"Nina?"

She squeaked, then some shuffles sounded from behind the fitting room's stall door. "Yeah?"

"Hurry it up. Let's go."

I turned to get back to the car, seething and rehearsing how I'd dissuade anyone from thinking I'd back my former friend in any future deals.

10

NINA

Nina

I nearly jumped out of my skin at Dante's rough order to move it. I didn't have much time to pick something suitable for Escott's, a fine establishment I never in a million years thought I'd go to. But the indecision I battled was fierce, worse than the pressing short deadline.

"I'm telling you," the boutique's employee said. She rolled her eyes so quickly I could've missed it. "Trust me on this. Get this one."

She was too pushy, likely wanting to make the commission on selling this designer gown. Her imploring me like that, to "trust" her, wasn't a show of sisterly advice given because she was an expert. It felt more like a joke. Like she was flaunting her supposed know-how that I lacked.

"I know it's probably not what you're familiar with…" She emphasized the dig by scooting past the chair where I'd placed my shirt and jeans. While Eva handled the online shopping for a new wardrobe to suit someone of the Constella caliber of wealth, I had yet to actually wear any of the designer garments. I had been sitting around reading at the mansion, not going anywhere with Dante to look good.

Until now.

His dinner "invitation" surprised me, but I'd known something would be coming.

However, my gut instinct about this so-called gown wouldn't quiet. I felt exposed, literally, with the deep cuts and flashiness of the clingy material. I felt out of my comfort zone, wearing this provocative dress. For dinner?

"I don't know…" I seldom showed myself off. My blouse and skirt combo of a waitress uniform was the extent of my ever dressing up. I was modest but unafraid of what I looked like. I just preferred not to emphasize my body for attention.

"It's classy," the attendant insisted. As she turned, she muttered, "Not that you would know."

She likely hadn't intended for me to overhear her. It proved that my instincts were right. This woman was just another mean girl, flagging me as inferior low class and unable to adjust to the fancy world of designer apparel. Or to know what was in style.

"Nina. Now." Dante came back to knock on the door and issue those two words. He didn't yell, but he didn't need to. His tone carried command, no matter what.

"All right." I shrugged and shook my head, hating that I had to surrender. Hearing Dante urged me to lose my stubbornness, though. This wasn't me. This dress wasn't. Going to Escott's wasn't. It was all a sham, so in that mindset, it didn't matter if I didn't feel comfortable in this damn dress.

I exited the stall, amazed and shocked at how easily such an outrageous dress could be bought with little more than a rich man's signature. Dante didn't look at me, his phone plastered to his ear as he led me back to the car, and I wondered what put him in a worse mood while I changed.

I didn't take that long. The store employee practically pushed that gown at me as soon as I told her we were going to Escott's for dinner.

While Dante drove, talking on the phone, I shrank into myself and tried to prepare for the evening. It was still a lot to adjust to, being with Dante and expected to act like his woman. On the way to the restaurant, I steadied my breath and braced for faking it.

Just be near him. Smile. And… follow his lead.

None of those thoughts helped. If I had to follow his lead, it would be sitting next to him while he paid attention to his phone.

Can I do this? Doubt crept in, and I tried to tug the hem of my dress lower on my thighs. Before this moment, it was easy. I'd been able to slowly relax in that guest room, feeling a little bit like a secret hidden away from the rest of the world. After a lifetime of working my ass off, those days of lying around and reading were a vacation.

Now, I felt cheap. Exposed in this dress. Clueless over how to look like I belonged with a sexy man like Dante. Outside his car that night I was lost in that bet, it was just the two of us kissing and talking. At a dinner with other men, I couldn't rely on a physical way of expressing our closeness—fake or not.

Too soon, we arrived, and as I took his hand and followed him inside, I worried he'd detect the slickness of my sweaty palm. I was nervous, so lost and confused.

I'd never gone to a fancy dinner. I'd never really dated! Neither of those scenarios were happening tonight, and the more I reminded myself that this was all an act, the more I could tune in to my objective.

Look like we're together. That was it. That was all I had to do.

And I tried.

Dante was in his element here, speaking with other equally wealthy and powerful men, none of whom I recognized. I doubted I'd remember their names, either, because I was the mute plus-one, not talked to or addressed past a hello. He mingled and spoke with many of them in this private dining room of the expensive place, and all I could do was trail along at his side and sip the drink I was handed.

He didn't hold my hand, but he made sure I stayed near him with glances to the side while he talked with the others. Nudging against my side, he reminded himself that we were in close proximity. All the while, he talked business.

The other men took more notice of me than Dante did, and every one of their lingering, leering, and studying looks bothered me. I hated how their glances got stuck on me—especially my exposed skin—and it reiterated how skimpy this dress was. It wasn't classy. It was revealing and daring.

Please, please look at me. Every time I caught Dante's distant gaze, I wished for him to turn his focus to me, even for a moment, to lend me his grounding presence. To remind me that even though it was all pretend and fake, we were here together.

The pre-dinner period wrapped up, and Dante turned toward me with a stern glower. He placed his hand on my elbow and steered me to the side, and I wondered why he looked so annoyed. He couldn't be mad at me. I'd done my part, being present and sticking to his side.

"What's wrong?" I didn't want to wait for him to discipline me or tell me why he was acting like I was bothering him. When he spoke with the other men, he was calm and collected, focused and attentive. With me, he was glaring and scowling.

"I don't like this," he admitted. "How they're…" His exhale was long and harsh. "They can't keep their fucking eyes off you."

Whether it was an attempt at flattery or irrational jealousy, he was far off the mark and had no room to blame me. I got dressed as I was told to. I showed up as he expected.

"Don't look at me like it's my fault," I snapped.

He dragged his angry gaze up and down me.

"I'm here playing the part, Dante." Keeping my voice to a whispered hush lowered the effectiveness of what I wanted to say. It was damned hard to yell at someone talking this quietly. "I'm dressed to be considered your arm candy, right?"

He looked away, annoyed.

"If you don't want them ogling me, then remind them that I'm here. With you. For you."

His stare was so dark and menacing, I regretted being so bold as to sass at him. But something about the shock in his eyes seemed a lot like a challenge, too. I wouldn't back down.

"Be with me if you want them to back off. Act like I'm with you."

Careful, Nina. Careful. This was supposed to be fake, but here I was talking like a whiny girlfriend who'd have an actual right to his attention. He wasn't interested. He'd made that clear, but I struggled not to blur the lines, wanting him to really notice me.

"All you've done is talk business." I lowered my gaze, too intimidated to keep up this direct eye contact. I couldn't read him, and I was nervous I'd pushed him too far.

His finger and thumb gripped my chin, and he tipped my face up so I'd see him.

"Be careful what you wish for," he growled.

I opened my mouth to retort something, but he slid his thumb up to snag my lower lip. "This is a business meeting."

"I know, but—"

"Dante," another man said, clapping him on the back as he approached.

Dante didn't take his gaze off me, not as he pulled me closer and turned with the man. We went to the table to eat. Our argument was cut short, but my words made an impact. Now, he held my hand. In the firm grip of his fingers wrapped around mine, I had a hunch he was going to prove me wrong.

Be careful what I wish for?

I bit my lip, wondering if he'd just issued a dare I wouldn't win. Because I wanted him—for real.

11

DANTE

Dante

"*Act like I'm with you.*"

If I could truly do that, we'd be giving them all too much of a show. I'd have my mouth over hers. My hands fisted in her hair. Her lipstick ruined and her body naked.

Giving myself the free rein to be with Nina would unleash a wave of desire no one could stop. Once I gave in to the lust she invoked, there would be no hiding or holding back.

However, after her words, I understood it from another perspective. She had done her part, getting dressed up and accompanying me, but as we took our seats for dinner, I replayed how much I'd actually interacted with her.

I hadn't.

At all.

With tunnel vision to counter the questions about what Stefan said, falsely claiming that the Constellas would always have his back in friendship and finances, I'd ignored Nina completely. The balance between paying attention to her and managing the business talk was off, and now it was time to make up for it.

She was right. If I wanted them to know I was with her, I had to act like it. And I started now. Holding her hand, speaking with her. Facing her and smiling at her nervousness.

I realized that she had likely been lost and confused, unsure how to act as my plus-one as I chatted with the men I often dealt with, leaders and capos of other families. Knowing she was suffering bothered me, and it prompted me to really give her all my attention.

The only catch was how much I wanted it to be real.

To act like I wanted her was a double-edged sword. Because I really did.

"More?" I offered after the dinner plates were cleared away. Holding up her empty glass, I suggested that she have more.

"Trying to loosen me up?" she teased with a small, sexy smile.

"Loosen?" I smirked. "I like how tight you are."

Her cheeks reddened immediately, and I fought a groan. Seeing her flushed like this was temptation personified. Knowing she was thinking about how I'd had my fingers in her pussy amused me. That was only the beginning of what I dreamed of doing to her, with her.

"Oh." Her quip of a reply was quiet and short, and I enjoyed rendering her speechless.

I paired it with grabbing her knee under the table, smoothing my fingers over her skin and wondering how far up her thigh I could touch her until she turned redder.

"Are you enjoying your evening?" I asked as I pushed my thumb and fingers along her leg.

She didn't stiffen, but I had a hunch she was measuring her breath carefully so as not to react too obviously to where my hand headed.

"I am." She swallowed, meeting my gaze directly. "I mean, now I am."

I hummed, accepting her jab. "Business always comes first," I reminded her.

"That's too bad." She parted her legs, widening her posture in her seat. The change in her angle gave me more access to slide my fingers further up smooth skin. And I didn't waste a second to do so. Leaning toward her, I stared right into her deep-blue eyes glittering with mischief. This slant made it obvious that I was feeling her up, and I didn't intend to hide it.

She was playing with fire to invite me to touch her more. I was burning up with the teasing thrill of trying to rile her up. This was far past flirting—real or fake. And as I gripped her chair and eased her onto my lap, I made sure that she knew it too.

"Oh. *Whoa.*" She exhaled in an unsteady whoosh, startled at how quickly and smoothly I put her where I wanted her. Merely holding hands and brushing up against each other was no longer enough. I had to get my hands on her, her body flush with mine.

I'd been resisting her all this time, but I knew she'd be able to feel the bulge under my pants. If I wasn't careful, I'd be tenting my pants sooner than later.

"Right now," I said as I nuzzled along her jaw and kissed her cheek, "I'd like to make sure *you* come first."

Her chest rose and fell faster as she leaned back to my chest, relaxed and open. Those generous tits nearly spilled out of her dress, and as I watched them, I was grateful her daring dress could be tugged down so easily. I wanted my fingers on her nipples, my mouth sucking on her flesh there.

She turned her head toward me, staring at me with such lust shining in her eyes. "Literally?" she whispered.

I answered by slipping my hand under her dress. The tablecloth hid most of her legs. The darkness of the dim dining room aided the shadows. Even if anyone could see that I wanted to feel her up, I wouldn't stop. I didn't care. This was taking "acting like it" too far, but it blended with what I wanted, anyway. Feeling her. Touching her. Pleasuring her.

"Do you want me to make you come?" I asked into her ear. I followed up with kissing along her jaw until I pressed against the corner of her mouth.

She moaned, turning the rest of the way until she kissed me. Deep and long. I growled into her kiss, and I anted up the tension by rubbing my fingers over her lingerie. The narrow strip of material would be wet soon enough, but for now, teasing her would do.

The idea of playing with her while the dinner concluded suited me. But I didn't want to share her. Seeing her come apart, hearing her come… I wanted to experience that alone. All for me.

But this is fake, right? Her desire wasn't. I knew she wanted me. She'd told her friend that. I felt the need in her as she kissed me back and kept her legs open for me to touch her.

It was difficult to separate what was an act from reality, but I refused to ease up on the torture and teasing.

"Dante?" Someone walked up to me, shaking his head as he glanced at his phone. "Since when are you agreeing to side with Giovanni about the distribution route to the ports?"

Fuck. They'd still been talking about Stefan and the shit he'd started to say.

"No." I stilled my hand under Nina's dress. She stiffened and held her breath, her mouth against my cheek. "You've got that wrong," I told the man from a rival yet not antagonist Mafia family.

"Huh. I heard…"

Just like that, I was taken down the path of talking business again. Nina remained on my lap, but I was pulled from giving her all my attention like I wanted to. Like I wished I could. Being intimate and close with her was a hell of a lot more exciting than talking business, but I tried my best to compromise. Keeping her on my lap, against me with my arms around her, I held up the image of us being all over each other and very much a couple. But as I chatted about Stefan and how I should not be assumed to be allying with him, I regretted the distractions of it all.

Nina distracted me from shooting down those rumors.

Stefan and his boisterous lies prevented me from making out with the young woman eager for my sensual guidance to be pleasured. It was a catch twenty-two of wanting her when I shouldn't. By the end of the night, I was frustrated with everything and anything.

Except her. Docile, quiet, and patient, Nina was an exemplary woman. She didn't huff and roll her eyes for not having all of my attention, nor did she interrupt or whine about being stuck there. It seemed that keeping physical contact with her went a long way toward assuaging her discomfort and feeling of being out of place, but it tormented me.

I wanted to rip this dress off her and fuck her senseless. I wanted to tell her to bend over and ride me in this chair, right here and now.

Instead, we managed to sit through the night—as a pair, man and woman together—until she excused herself.

"I'll be right back." She kissed my cheek, and I loved how at ease she was with touching me and showing affection—although under the guise of faking it.

She stood, but I kept my hands on her waist as she got to her feet.

"Just running to the bathroom," she explained with a sweet smile just for me.

"I'll be waiting for you." I watched her until she disappeared from sight through the doorway. Once she was gone, I exhaled long and hard.

"Damn. What a fine piece of ass," Leo, a high-ranking capo from another family, said.

I shot him a hard look. "She's not. Not a piece of ass."

Nina was my old friend's daughter, and I hated to hear anyone belittle her as easy pussy, dime a dozen and nothing special.

"Oh. It's serious, then?" Leo asked, taking Nina's absence as a break from whatever business we'd been talking about. "You and her?" He sipped his drink. "Hell, it's only been twenty years since Grace died."

"Thirty," I corrected, missing Nina already. Leo wouldn't be talking about my dead first wife if she were here, and I didn't like going down memory lane that far.

"And here I thought it'd be you and Vanessa pairing up," Leo teased with a knowing look.

"No." I said it firmer than I intended to, but I couldn't restrain from blurting out the instant reply to that line. "I've made it more than clear that I'm not interested in anything with Vanessa. Nor her father."

Leo nodded. "Nothing with the Giovannis at all."

"That's correct."

How many times will I need to tell them? Stefan had always been a talker, loud and obnoxious, but no matter how much he spouted bullshit about having Constella backing, I'd reject it all.

I fell back into talking about business, but unlike the pre-dinner mingling hour, this post-dinner session of talking and drinking felt lonely. I wanted Nina back at my side, and I realized with another glance at my watch that she'd been gone for quite a while. If she wanted a breath of fresh air outside, whatever. Guards waited at the doors, and they would protect her. No MC biker would dare come to Escott's, but I'd made it clear to all the Constella men that Nina was under my protection.

"Excuse me." I left the dining room and sought her out, curious whether it had all been too much for her. I struggled between wanting her and telling myself that I shouldn't, and I imagined she felt the same.

"Nina?" I called out for her as I walked through the room and strode down the hallways to reach where the restrooms were. Nothing could have prepared me for the sight I found.

Nina, pressed against the wall. One man with his hand over her mouth, silencing her as his friend groped her, yanking her dress down.

They were servers, men who'd waited on us in the private dining room. I didn't know what made them so deluded to act on their lust for her as she walked alone to the restrooms. I didn't care, either. Rabid rage swarmed through me. My blood pressure skyrocketed. My pulse raced. Fisting my hands, I hurried closer to free her and make these stupid bastards pay for even thinking about touching her.

Romeo appeared, though. He'd arrived too late for the dinner but had just begun to make his rounds with the men as they drank and talked business.

He strode toward the men faster than I could reach them.

"What the fuck do you think you are doing?" he roared, yanking them off her.

She staggered back against the wall, slinking out of reach. Her wide-open eyes conveyed the depth of her fear. Trembling lips, pale face, and hunching over, she was the picture of a terrified woman.

Anger rallied higher. My need to hurt them grew and grew. I wanted to comfort her, but I couldn't be any good at that while these men lived and breathed.

"Take her home," I ordered my son. Two Constella guards rushed in, likely nearby because both of us were here.

Romeo, panting hard, turned back to see me. Then he looked at Nina, shrinking back against the wall.

"Take her home," I ordered as the soldiers grabbed both of the waiters.

Romeo shook his head. "I can—"

"You can take Nina home. Now." I spared her a glance, not meaning to glare at her with this feral fury. As I handed another soldier my jacket, I let the heat of my rage and possessiveness over her keep me warm.

She wasn't mine. Not really. It was only supposed to be fake. The idea of these assholes pawing at her guaranteed that they'd die a slow, painful death at my hands, though. And the faster I did that, the sooner I could comfort her and make sure she wouldn't be too scarred from the trauma of this evening.

"Go," I ordered.

"Dante." She stepped toward me, perhaps even more frightened with the rage I couldn't hold back. "I didn't—"

"For fuck's sake." I shook my head as the soldiers dragged the waiters outside. "I know, Nina." That she could assume I would blame her for any of this was ridiculous. "I know you didn't do anything."

All she'd done since running into me was agree to fake date me. Right now, I had to punish these men for daring to touch what was mine, pretend or not. Because I had a very serious issue of seeing Nina as mine.

And no man would live to touch what I called mine. Ever.

12

NINA

Nina

After a week of hiding at Dante's mansion and waiting for him to need me to act like his girlfriend, this roller coaster of a night threw me off.

"This way," Romeo said as he ushered me toward a car.

I hadn't seen Dante's son in years. Many, many years, but I recognized the boy he once was in the man who led me out of Escott's and to an SUV with blacked-out windows.

"Yeah," I replied breathlessly, worn from the rush to flee and the speediness of how things had changed so quickly.

The expectation to get ready to play pretend for the dinner. Dante's blinders to my presence before dinner. The extreme opposite of his affection and kisses after it.

And then those two waiters finding me in the hallway, lost on my way to the restrooms because this place was enormous. They capitalized on the fact that I was alone, and with two of them, taller and stronger, I was outnumbered.

Fear and anger meshed, but it ended up as an overwhelming sense of panic.

If Romeo hadn't arrived when he had.

If Dante hadn't come to find me…

Shuddering at how closely I'd come to being violated—or worse, raped—was a hell of a hit to come down from. My skin stung, bleeding slightly from their nails when they clawed at my dress. My cheek burned from the backhand the taller guy gave me when I threatened to scream. Warm liquid trickled over my cheek. It wasn't a tear, but a spot of blood. They'd broken my flesh, and the physical reminder of what happened somehow grounded me. Pressing my fingers to the cut was a motion that helped to pull me from sinking into my head.

"Thank—" I swallowed, then cleared my throat. My mouth was still too dry to speak as I followed Romeo to the passenger door. "Thank you. For…"

"You're welcome." He opened the door, frowning at me as I held up the torn scrap of fabric that those waiters tugged from my neck. "Here."

He didn't need to open the door any farther. Constella guards flanked us, and more stood behind me. They were a wall, surely protecting me from Escott's. With how unsettled and weary I was, I would've wedged myself through a slim gap of the door's opening. I wanted to get out of there—now.

But what about Dante? I paused long enough to cast a worried glance back at the building. I wasn't scared for him. He could handle those men. Dante was older, stronger, more muscled. But I couldn't shake the anxiety sinking in.

"I didn't encourage them," I told Romeo as soon as he got in the car and put it in gear. "I didn't... I didn't do anything. I was just going to the bathroom and they cornered me and—"

He lifted his hand to gesture for me to stop. "No one's blaming you for anything."

"Okay. But I just wanted to say it."

He huffed a dark laugh as he loosened his tie. The Romeo from my childhood was always a serious boy, but the man he'd become wasn't any different. His aura, his presence, was a somber, serious one. "I came to the dinner late, but I noticed them checking you out."

I frowned, watching his profile.

Glancing at me but keeping his focus primarily on the road, he seemed just as confused as I felt. "You were... watching me?"

"It's been a long fucking time since I've seen you, but yeah, I watched you. Or I guess I noticed you." At a red light, he studied me. "It's been an even longer time since my father actually dated someone or brought a date to anything. So, yeah, color me surprised to see him at dinner with a woman."

I winced. Dante struggled with the act of having a woman in his life, and Romeo's wording made me wonder if the sexy man was really that clueless and rusty.

"He hasn't dated anyone since my mother died."

"Whoa." I blinked, not expecting that. She passed away before I was even born, so that was one long dry spell. As handsome and attractive as Dante was—not to mention his obvious expertise in pleasing a woman—I knew he hadn't been celibate all this time. Yet, I didn't know how to interpret his breaking his dry spell with me.

"You're with him now?" he asked. His tone was similar to Dante's. Firm and with authority. I had to answer.

"Um, yes."

He shook his head, chuckling to himself. "I shouldn't bother asking. I saw enough."

You saw us all over each other because we were faking it.

"I'm pretending to be with him." I cringed as soon as the words left my lips. Blurting that out was dumb. The only way Dante and I could fake this relationship was if we kept it a secret. I already told Tessa. She wouldn't blab about it, but Romeo?

I didn't know if he could be trusted with this secret. Or if Dante would be mad that I'd told him, too. Romeo and I had never really gotten along. He was too serious. I was too quiet. We seldom saw each other, only during those few times my dad visited and brought us along when he caught up with Dante.

"Are you trying to manipulate him?" Romeo demanded.

"No! No." I shook my head, trying to pull the torn dress up higher on my chest. "Not him. We're both pretending."

"You're pretending to be together." He said it instead of asking it. "No. I don't buy that."

"What?" I furrowed my brow, worried that I'd opened my mouth at all and that he seemed to think I could be trying to con his father. "No. It's true."

"He's pretending that you're his girlfriend?" He looked at me before pulling off the highway.

"Yes."

"You?"

I groaned. "What? I'm not fake-girlfriend quality?"

"That's not my call to make. All I'm saying is that I don't believe you. I saw you at the restaurant. You were all over each other."

"Because we were pretending."

"Yeah, right." He chuckled once again, annoyed as he shook his head. "If that's the line you're sticking with, you might want to consider that he's more interested in you than you think."

"He's…" I thought back to his kisses. His touches. Maybe he was that focused and driven to always be in business mode that he'd forgotten how to act like he had a date. Once I pointed it out to him, he was touching me and doting on me.

Be careful what you wish for. Did he really mean that he'd deliver on it?

"He's not." I cleared my throat. "He's not interested in me for real. We just want to make it believable, and with how obsessed he is with work matters and whatnot, it simply looked convincing."

"That's what you think?" He smirked at me.

I had no clue what to think anymore.

"Why would you need to pretend to date anyone? Much less, my dad?"

"I was lost in a bet to the Devil's Brothers club."

He raised his brows. "What?"

I sighed, embarrassed to admit it. Romeo and I had never really gotten along. He was older than me, but while Ricky was closer in age to him, their birthdays uncannily close to each other, they'd never gotten along well, either. Romeo was just too serious of a person to get close with.

"Ricky bet on me with Reaper, the bikers' leader, and lost. Your dad suggested that we pretend to date so the MC guys would back off. That if they saw me with him, they'd realize I was already taken."

"Goddamn." He rolled his eyes. "Your brother is a fucking dumbass."

I shrugged. I wouldn't argue with him there. In fleeting moments, it made my blood pressure spike with the reminders of how he'd treated me like a thing to toss around.

"Seriously. He's a moron to even try to negotiate or deal with that MC."

I pursed my lips together as he pulled into the driveway. I didn't know what to tell him, and it seemed he wasn't waiting for a response, anyway.

When I reached for the door handle, he got out and rounded the front of the car.

"Right. I'm supposed to be a delicate, pampered lady unable to open a damn door," I mumbled to myself, somehow peeved by this gentlemanly gesture the Constella man insisted on. It probably annoyed me because I'd grown up without such simple shows of chivalry, but now wasn't the time to stress about it.

Romeo assisted me out of the car and led me up to the front door. "You'll be all right here?"

"I, um… He moved me in here Monday."

"Oh." He looked at the door, opening it. "I haven't been staying here lately. So, news to me. Will you be all right?" Only now did he glance down at my chest where the men ripped my dress and scraped my skin. When he lifted his gaze to the small scrape on my cheek, he clenched his jaw, murderous at the reminder that I'd nearly been violated.

"George can arrange assistance," he added.

I shook my head. "I can slap a Band-Aid on. I'll be all right." Truthfully, I doubted I would be until I saw Dante again, but I wouldn't go there. I didn't want to think about what he might be doing, looking so sinister and malicious while those two waiters were dragged away.

I knew this was a Mafia family, but right now, I hated to consider the violence happening by the man I was pretending to date.

"I can…" Romeo turned back after nodding at me. He returned to me just inside the foyer. "I can set up some self-defense lessons for you. If you'd like. I know what you mean about him. My dad often gets into his business mode and struggles to see anything beyond it. His work has been his life for too long. If he neglects to show you how to fend off men, if any punks ever dare to bother you like those two men did tonight, you can be trained and prepared."

I opened and closed my mouth, at a loss for what to say. For as serious and solemn as Romeo was, he was considerate, too. "Really?"

He nodded, unsmiling and sincere. "Yes."

"Okay. Um, yeah. Thank you. I would like that." I nodded once. "I appreciate that."

With one last look, he turned and left me.

Romeo's offer to show me the basics of self-defense was a gift I could rely on well after this fake-dating ruse was up with Dante. That simple suggestion of protection meant a lot to me, especially after the fact that my brother lost me in a bet and had been prepared to hand me over to rough bikers.

I'd never been protected. Not from life, not from punks or assholes. Sure, men groped me when I waitressed, but tonight was a striking turning point. I'd almost been raped, and being saved by Romeo, then Dante, I felt treasured and secure.

Instead of seeking out George or Eva, or any of the staff here, I trudged upstairs to clean up.

This night hadn't gone like I thought it might. It'd ended on a lousy note.

But as I let myself into my guest room, I rolled my eyes at the absurdity that Romeo acted like the big brother I'd never had in Ricky.

And to make it even weirder? I was dating his dad.

"No." I closed the door and sighed. "No, I'm not."

I was fake dating Dante, and I winced at how hard it was to reinforce the distinction.

13

DANTE

Dante

Torturing the two servers didn't take long. The faster I killed them at the building my soldiers took them to, it was that much sooner that I could go home and check on Nina.

As I beat them to bloody pulps before shooting them, I realized the first mistake I'd made.

One of two crucial mistakes.

By asking Nina to pretend to be my girlfriend, I'd made her a target. Any significant other of a Mafia leader would be targeted for an attack, kidnapping, or rape. Aside from the Devil's Brothers MC looking for her, any of my enemies could also try to reach her and hurt her. Fake or not, once people realized Nina was "mine", she could be taken or hurt.

These two servers weren't operating from a rival family. They were merely that stupid, commoners who wanted to rape a woman by herself.

It was wrong of me to ever let her get near danger, and I loathed that she had been touched at all.

"I will do better, Nina," I said as I drove myself home after leaving my men to dispose of the bodies. "I will." She deserved the best, and if it meant managing a better balance between my business expectations and seeing to her comfort, I would do it.

While I killed those men, though, I recognized my other error. It was a fool's errand thinking Nina and I could make this fake relationship believable without it impacting us.

I wanted her. I wanted to make her feel safe and secure just the same as I longed to pleasure her and push her to bliss.

All of it. I desired her more than I should, and as I arrived at the house and hurried to find her, I wondered how long I could deny myself—and her.

"Nina?" I knocked but didn't wait for her reply before opening her door. She never locked it, and I took it as another sign of her innocence and willingness to accommodate me here. She was a guest but felt like so much more.

"Nina? I—" I stopped short, finding her in the bathroom attached to her guest suite.

There she was, wearing a top and short shorts as her body shook at the large vanity. Scrubbing something lying on the long counter, she mumbled to herself quietly, oblivious that I'd come in.

"Nina."

She startled, turning around partly with a gasp. "Oh! Dante."

I huffed a little laugh. Expecting someone else?

I didn't miss how she glanced at my hands, likely expecting them to be bloody.

"Are you all right?"

Her reply was a shrug. She turned back to the counter and resumed scrubbing. "Yeah, sure. They didn't actually…"

"Don't downplay it," I warned her as I walked up to her.

"I'm not. I'm just saying they didn't really touch me or do anything. Romeo walked by before they could. And you." She frowned, soaking a small cloth again.

Wet smears showed on the fabric, and with the redder spots in the middle of the area, it was clear that she was trying to remove a blood stain.

Whose?

I laid my hand on hers, ceasing her frantic attempt to clean the material. She slowly lifted her gaze to me, and with that move, she turned toward me. It gave me a chance to see her torso. The tank top she'd put on was cut low enough that I saw the small scrape on her chest. A faint mark showed on her cheek, too, and the visuals of her in any kind of pain renewed the anger that had started to dissipate when I killed the men who'd touched her.

"It's not bad," she said.

"I told you." I lowered my fingers to tip her chin up, taking in the full, clear sight of her scrapes. She didn't flinch or shy away, letting me see. "Any mark on you is a crime."

She'd showered. The steam hung in the air yet, and her hair was still damp, lying in a sexy mess over her shoulders and down her back. The cuts were cleaned, but I wished they could be erased altogether.

"I'm sorry."

"No. This isn't your fault."

I cleared my throat and shoved the dress aside. Before she could reach for it, I picked her up and set her on the edge of the counter.

"Wait." She stretched her hand out toward it, but I didn't let her take it. "I can clean that out and sew the strap and it'll be as good as new."

I bit the inside of my cheek, determined not to humor her with a smile. This adorable woman. She wanted to repair the damn gown and make sure it still had value?

"Why?"

"Well, I could resell it for a lot of money. It's a waste to just throw it away."

I sighed, sliding the first-aid kit closer. She must have set it out but had prioritized cleaning and salvaging the dress over seeing to her wounds. I knew she wasn't materialistic, but her words and scrappiness endeared her to me.

Nina wasn't like other Mafia women. She wasn't used to fineries and wealth. If I'd been looking for a materialistic girlfriend, Nina wasn't it. After years of the same old, she was a refreshing change. I didn't have to worry about what she'd try to get out of me, and that was a freedom I seldom faced.

"Forget it."

She nodded but frowned as she watched me open the kit and find the antibiotic cream and bandages. "Oh. No. Dante, I can do that."

I leaned closer, standing between her knees, and that approach had her flinching on the counter.

"Easy."

She rubbed the back of her neck, reluctant to make eye contact all of a sudden. After the night she'd had, I wasn't shocked that she was skittish. But it seemed like she was nervous around me, not that she was traumatized by those men.

"I'm sorry that this happened," I said as I began to tend to the scrape on her chest. Having my fingers near her breasts messed with me.

While there was nothing sexy about the motions of helping her with basic first aid, it felt intimate.

Being alone together. Granted the permission to touch her...

"It's life," she replied. "It's not the first time I was groped or someone grabbed at me."

I narrowed my eyes at her, hating that this was her reality. "Where?"

"Mainly at the Hound and Tea."

"When you were working?"

She nodded, then held still as I smeared the cream on the small cut on her cheek. "I share that with you. Work. It was all I ever did. So, if men got handsy, it was just part of the job. Happens to women everywhere."

I glanced into her blue eyes, holding her gaze for a few seconds. "Not anymore."

"Well, yeah. Because I don't work there right now. Since I'm here... With you."

I loathed how temporary that sounded. It was becoming all too easy and natural to come home and know she would be here in my house.

"And because if another man ever touches you again, he'll die at my hands, just like those two servers did."

I watched her delicate throat flex with her struggle to swallow. Then meeting her eyes, I waited for a sign of horror or disgust. I saw none.

Instead, she sighed. "I figured as much."

"Figured what?" I pressed the small bandages to her cuts.

"That you'd hurt them."

I helped her down. "I killed them, Nina." I didn't need to tell her, but I wanted to. She was so damn different from me and what I was used to. She was new, ignorant about the ins and outs of the Mafia lifestyle. She was poor and inexperienced, not having lived through much yet in her life. Those contrasts between us only made me want her more, and I felt obligated to test her on this. To see if her knowing I killed someone—on her behalf—would make her feel repulsed by me.

Standing still, as I kept my hands on her hips, she nodded. "Yeah. I figured that."

"And it doesn't bother you?"

She licked her lips. "No? I have no control over you or what you say and do. You live by a different code, and it's not my place to judge or expect anything otherwise."

Urging her to leave the bathroom, I walked with her. "Is this your way of saying 'you do you'?"

"Maybe?" She bit her lower lip and dropped her gaze. "I just don't understand why you'd go to such lengths."

I guided her toward the bed. Once we were there, I pulled the cover back and gestured for her to get in. I'd done what I came here to do. I checked on her. She seemed fine. I satisfied myself in tending to her cuts.

But I had to get the fuck out of here. She was skittish around me, not playful or flirty like she had been at the restaurant. I wanted her like that again, but I had no right to wish for it.

Not here. Not alone, with her trusting and open, following my lead and acting so submissive.

I'd fuck her—all night, every way possible. But that was so far from "faking it" that it couldn't happen.

"I'm not… yours," she said as she climbed onto the bed and gazed up at me.

"Everyone is supposed to think that, though."

"So you avenged me because of our fake connection?" She arched one brow, putting me on the spot.

If she was fishing, if she was testing the waters to see if I'd tell her that she mattered for real, she'd be waiting a long time. I was doing my best to keep myself in check, and I would last longer yet.

I couldn't cave to her. At least not yet. She looked to me for protection. If she were really my woman, she'd be in a bigger world of danger, targeted as collateral. And I hated the possibility of her ever being hurt again.

"I will always do everything in my power to make sure you are safe, Nina."

She sighed again, but it morphed into a yawn. "I'm sorry. For not holding up my end of the bargain very well."

I scowled at her sexy, relaxed position on the bed. Even though we spoke slowly, calmly, and quietly, my heart raced and my dick hardened. This was a gentler moment that we shared here, but dammit, did I want to join her on this bed and really make her forget about what happened earlier.

"How can you say that? How are you not holding up your end well? All those men knew that you were with me. That was the whole point."

"I know. But..." She shrugged and smiled so faintly and quickly that I knew she was holding back on replying with what was really on her mind. "Forget it. Never mind." Ever so slightly, she gave me a doe-eyed, submissive expression that tempted me. Like she wanted to tell me without a single word that she desired me.

Oh, Nina... I want to.

Her sexy, seductive gaze was a plea, a desperate beg for me to join her in this bed. Maybe she was too timid. Perhaps she didn't know how to ask for it and hoped I'd read the message on her expressive, beautiful face.

I did. But I resisted.

Instead, I tested my patience and control. Dipping in closer, I kissed her brow then retreated before I could dare to lay my lips on her anywhere else.

"Good night."

The disappointment in her eyes irked me, but I knew I couldn't cave. It wouldn't help either of us. "Good night, Mr. Constella," she remarked cheekily, but sleepily.

I smirked, standing straight before turning to leave.

As soon as I exited her room, I hesitated in the hallway. I adjusted my erection beneath my pants, growling lightly at how hard she'd made me.

One glance at her closed door taunted me. It was unlocked. It was always unlocked. She lay in there, gazing up at me with such openness and trust. All I would have to do would be to walk back in and have my way with her.

Though it wasn't easy, I resisted my desire and strode away before I could act on this damning, hexing connection that had yet to fade.

I'd killed for her.

Reaching my room and knowing I'd need to shower and jerk off to a fantasy of her, I knew I'd do anything for the woman I was supposed to pretend was mine.

14

NINA

Nina

My scrapes healed within a few days. While it was scary to be caught by two men, no lasting trauma bothered me past that first night. It was like I told Dante. Men preyed on women all the time. That wasn't any excuse, claiming it was the status quo to tolerate and get used to, but there was nothing I could do to change the general mindset the everyday, common men held against women.

Being caught by the bikers and handed over to Reaper *did* scare me, and as long as I remained in this fake relationship with Dante, I was safe. I'd avoid that fate for as long as I could.

Instead of going back to how it was that first week, Dante was more present. At least in passing. He was still busy—always on the phone or taking off to talk with people. Several times, I spotted him meeting with Franco and Romeo near the pool. The one day I walked out there, prepared to swim, I found them seated at a table under a large umbrella. I'd never wrapped myself back up in a towel and bolted back into the house faster than that moment. My bathing suit wasn't too skimpy, but it wasn't the definition of modesty, either. I simply felt bad that I might have interrupted.

After that incident, though, it seemed like Dante was *trying* to encounter me in his massive house. He came home to eat dinner with me. We didn't speak. Franco and I carried on chatting the little that we did since he was at the house more than Dante. Still, Dante was there.

And again, when I headed to the gym, I passed him while exiting it. Another time when I wanted a snack, we bumped into each other near the kitchen. They all seemed like innocent episodes of happenstance. If I believed in coincidences, I would've claimed that was the case for our run-ins.

Maybe he was planning it. I didn't know. But in the week following that dinner, when I told him to act like he wanted to be with me, I wondered if he thought I meant it literally.

"He has to know that I meant it in terms of the pretending to date scenario," I told Tessa on the phone. "Right?"

"I don't know."

I gnawed on my lower lip, heading downstairs to make lunch for myself. Maybe Romeo or Franco would stop through and I could whip up a sandwich and salad for them. Dante told me just yesterday that I didn't need to put my foot forward and contribute to the household. He reminded me that they hired staff to keep the house running. But I'd gotten used to being here and feeling like I was "with" the Constellas, and it was natural to want to share a lunch with the others.

"When I put him on the spot and said he had to act like he wanted to be near me to make this fake dating believable, he told me to be careful what I wished for," I told her.

"*Ooh*. Sounds naughty."

"But he was joking." He had to be. "This sexual tension between us hasn't faded, but he took an out from acting on it. That night, he saw me to bed, and there is *no* way he missed how I was looking at him."

"How?" she asked.

"Like I wanted him to devour me. Like I wanted to devour him. Horny, Tessa. I was turned on from how he'd been acting earlier, and I looked like a horny woman who wanted his fine ass."

"The night that those guys cornered you?" she asked, incredulous. "Of course, he didn't take you up on any sexy time. You'd just been scared."

Not really. I knew that Dante was in the building, that Constella guards were near. *It was also the night that he cared so much about what happened that he killed those two men.*

"It's just so confusing now." Half the time, I thought he wanted me, and the other half, I was convinced that he wanted to be married to his businesses and organization with no time to spare for anything or anyone else. "All these encounters and happening to bump into each other."

"Well, what do you expect? You're living there like roommates already."

I guessed I was expecting that he'd treat me like he did before, that mixture of teasing me and wanting me but keeping his distance anyway.

Eva strode through the first floor, her narrowed gaze settled on me. Like every other time I saw Eva in his huge house, I prepared for another bit of the mean-girl act. It was clear that she disliked me. While I wouldn't hold it against her for being protective of her uncle and cousin, she had to learn to back off. I wasn't here to ruin them. I didn't want to cause issues with anyone.

She seemed impervious to understanding that, no matter how polite and open I was with her.

"I'll call you later," I told Tessa. I didn't need Eva hearing about my mixed feelings about Dante. As far as she knew, I was his girlfriend whom he seldom gave attention to.

"Call with your lover?" Eva guessed.

Why can't you go back to the other house? I just didn't want to deal with her. Those first few days, she helped get me a wardrobe and necessities, where she assumed I was a poor nobody to provide for. Maybe that was the reason for her defensiveness. She assumed I was taking advantage of Dante's wealth.

If he were my sugar daddy, that would sum it up.

On her tour, she pointed out the extravagant guest house that she called home on the property. Romeo lived in another.

After those initial days, though, I didn't have to put up with her much.

"No, Eva." I sighed, peeved that she'd test me and accuse me of having a lover. The only man I wanted to label as that was Dante. More and more, I dreamed and fantasized about him.

"Would you like to have lunch with me?" I offered, determined to act like the bigger person, killing hatred with kindness and all.

"No." She crossed her arms, looking me up and down and no doubt annoyed that I still wore the clothes *I* picked, generic, casual clothes, not the designer crap she had delivered here for me.

The bell rang before she could speak another word. I glanced toward the front door, then wondered if George would get it. I wasn't prohibited from ever opening the door, but no one ever rang the bell. Everyone who came here had to be approved by the men at the gates, and everyone who fell in that category typically parked and entered the house through the garage connection.

"Who's that?" I asked her.

"What, am I a psychic now? I have no clue." Eva smirked at me. "Did you invite someone over?"

Argh! Stop already. "No, I haven't." I didn't know the damn address to give to anyone.

"Should I wait for George?" I asked her.

"God, you're so clueless. He's off today. He has a doctor appointment."

I nodded, wincing. "Right. That root canal appointment." I shrugged, striding toward the door and hoping it was nothing I'd need to deal with. My stomach growled, and I would get hangry at any second since I worked out hard this morning downstairs.

After I undid the locks and put my faith in the fact that no one could come here without passing the gates, then also the perimeter guards patrolling the perimeter, I pulled open one half of the old double doors.

A slim brunette stood there expectantly. Her sneer suggested disdain at seeing me answering. Despite the breeze in the air, her styled hair remained perfect and smooth, in place. Beneath her expertly applied makeup, her skin glowed, but the too-puffy lips she curled in annoyance were so fake that I wondered if she could tell she was moving them.

"Hello?"

Her face twisted some more, contorting her cringe into a grimace. "Excuse me?"

What? I raised my brows. "Hello?"

"Why aren't you in uniform?" she demanded.

"Uniform?" I glanced to the side, catching Eva's eye. She remained to my right, out of sight from this visitor at the door. Rolling her eyes and crossing her arms, she stayed out of it.

"I don't have a uniform," I said slowly, wondering if she was unhinged or lost. "Can I help you?"

"Aren't you a housekeeper?"

I sighed, losing patience. "No. I'm not. No solicitors, please." Slowly closing the door, I chalked this off as an oddity. How a saleslady got past security was beyond me.

"What?" She slammed her hand on the door, keeping it open. "I'm not selling anything." She held a bag up. The crinkly paper sticking out of the container showed that it was a baked good of some kind from a fancy bakery. "I'm here to see Dante."

"You are?"

She huffed. "Yes. For our lunch date."

I narrowed my eyes. If anyone could be claiming a date with that man, it would've been me. Falsely, in the name of make-believe, but still. He was *mine*.

"No, you're not."

She dropped her jaw. "*Excuse* me?"

I set one hand on my hip. "You're not here for any date with him."

"Says who?"

I shot her an amused look. "Me."

"Who the hell are you?"

"His girlfriend."

For several minutes, she laughed so hard that tears leaked out of her eyes. I stood there, waiting until she calmed down. Trying to shove inside, she shook her head. "Get out of my way."

I slapped my hand on the doorframe and locked my elbow. It served as a very physical blockade that prevented her from coming any closer.

"No."

"You are not his girlfriend." She shook her head, like the joke was on me.

I stared her down. If she was looking for a pushover, she wouldn't find one now in me. I wasn't Dante's anything, not really, but this was the role he expected me to carry out. I had no idea who this woman was, so I bet I had to maintain this falsehood with her, too.

"He's waiting for me," she insisted hotly.

He's not even here, idiot. He'd left an hour ago, stopping in the gym when I was halfway through my workout to tell me he was going to a meeting. At that time, I was surprised but touched that he told me anything.

"You don't have to report in to me," I'd teased, sweaty and gross on the treadmill.

He'd simply shoved his hands in his pockets and shrugged. "Maybe I want to."

More confusing words.

"He's not waiting for you," I told the woman at the door. "And he's not interested in your gift." I looked at the bakery bag in her hand.

"I don't know who the fuck you think you are," she snarled, "but he's not with you or anyone but—"

I slammed the door in her face. Since a scream of pain didn't follow, I assumed she reared back out of the way before it literally hit her in the nose. Curses and shouts came muffled through the door, but I was done. If she kept up that noise, a guard would escort her off the property.

I was too damn hungry to bother with it. Turning to head to the kitchen again, I slowed my steps at Eva's mocking slow clap.

"Nice to see you're not a pushover."

I looked at her, not betraying my emotions. If I didn't engage with her cattiness, I was sure she'd go away sooner or later.

"You stood your ground." She followed me, not giving up on my speedy walk to the kitchen.

"Vanessa's never pleasant to put up with, but slamming the door in her face..." She laughed darkly as I reached the kitchen and opened the fridge. "That was brilliant."

"Vanessa, huh?" I asked as I peered in the fridge. Now I had a name. The next time I ran into Dante in the house, I'd make sure to ask him what the hell was up with her stopping by like that.

"Yeah. Vanessa Giovanni. You sure showed her."

I shrugged. Dante gave me a role, to act as his girlfriend, and I damn well would follow through with it. "Want a salad?" I glanced back at Eva now. She stood with her hip propped against the edge of the island's counter.

She exhaled, like she was bracing for saying something more. "Nina, why *are* you dating Dante?"

I mentally groaned, not wanting the third degree again. She bombarded me with all kinds of questions about our relationship, but fortunately, Dante overheard her and set her straight with vague answers.

"Because I can't blame Vanessa for laughing at the idea of your dating my uncle."

I huffed as I set veggies on the counter. "Gee. Thanks."

"Nothing personal," she said.

"Oh, I'm sure it is."

"You're just not his type. That's a fact." As I looked up at her, she raised her brows, haughty like a know-it-all. "You are not Dante's type—at all. Yet you're here."

I did jazz hands, just to piss her off. "Here I am," I sing-songed. "That's a no on a salad, then?"

"No. No salad. Nina, why is my uncle wasting his time dating *you*?" She stared at me directly, giving me no option to hedge the question.

I bit my lip, tempted to just tell her. That I *wasn't* dating him, although I wished I were, so badly. That I yearned for his kisses and missed his seductive, filthy looks.

While I blurted out the truth to Romeo and admitted that Dante and I were pretending to be together, I was nervous to share that same uncensored truth with her. I didn't know if I could trust Eva, and I wasn't confident or brave enough to take a leap of faith and try to. I still wondered if I was wrong to confide in Romeo the little that I had, but so far, nothing had come back to me from that. Dante hadn't come to me, demanding to know why I told his son the truth.

Besides, what the hell can I say? Oh, I'm here because he wants me to look like his girlfriend. It's supposed to be an act, but I really wish it were the truth.

My desire for Dante was only deepening, and I realized my interest in him was like a ticking bomb. The longer I faked it, that I was merely here to pretend, the more my affections solidified and strengthened.

Sooner or later, something would snap. Something would have to give.

But I wasn't giving Eva a morsel of truth now.

"Because he wants to date me." I shot her a flat look that warned her that I wouldn't say another damn word about it.

15

DANTE

Dante

Franco joined me at one of the family's restaurants, and I wondered when I could plan to bring Nina here. Ever since that night at Escott's, I wanted another opportunity to take her out. To be seen with her. To have an excuse to show her off and demonstrate that she was my woman.

I'd damned myself by reminding her that we only had to "put the show on" when others were near.

All week long, I'd been going out of my way to see her. To pass her by. Even a quick hello in the house.

That night at Escott's changed something. Not because I'd killed those men for touching her.

But because she'd offered herself to me and I turned her down.

"Romeo should be here any minute," Franco said as our drinks arrived.

I shrugged. I wasn't Romeo's keeper. He was my second in command and never failed me. However... "He's still out of sorts about Mario betraying us."

Franco's sigh was heavy and long. "I don't think he's upset and guilty about Mario turning rat. Only that three soldiers were killed and he wasn't quick enough to save them."

I nodded, angry and proud at the same time. I loathed losing good men too, but I wanted Romeo to move past it all somehow. I was glad I'd done a decent job raising him on my own. He was always so serious, but big-hearted too. If he'd dismissed those deaths like they meant nothing, then he'd be nothing more than another cold-blooded killer.

He showed up, halting us from talking about him any further. "Sorry." He shook his head. "Stopped by the house and got delayed."

The house? Did something happen with Nina? "How come?"

He rolled his eyes. "Eva."

Enough said. My niece could get into a mother-hen mood no one was spared from.

"Did you see that message?" Romeo asked Franco.

Franco grimaced, showing me his phone. "I did. Look, Dante."

I glanced at the small screen, seeing the same image that another soldier had already sent to me. "I was updated about this already. Those goddamn bikers," I groused.

A Constella soldier had captured video and still images of a biker speaking with one of Stefan's leading capos.

"They're talking about that guns distribution route," Franco said. "That's gotta be why they risked meeting up like this."

I shook my head. We would have absolutely nothing to do with it. No matter how many rumors Stefan spread, he wouldn't include me. I wouldn't enter any deal with those bikers.

"I looked into them," Romeo said with a glance at me. "After Nina mentioned them in passing, that Ricky was friends with them…"

Fuck. Did he know? Romeo wasn't stupid, but he had yet to ask me about Nina being at the house.

"They're a nasty bunch of assholes," he summed up.

"We already knew that when they declared war against the Domino Family," I reminded him.

"Declared war and won," Franco added. "Maybe they're scheming with the Giovannis to attack someone else."

I met and held his gaze. "If they make us their enemies…" I shook my head. "They won't survive." The Constella Family had reigned supreme for too long for some newcomers like filthy, gritty bikers to throw us out of power.

"All the more reason to track their meetings and keep up on spying on them," Franco said. "I've already delegated more men to the threats."

I grunted. "Not a threat yet." *But the moment they do strike out, in any direction near us, they'll be greeted with as much ammunition as we have.*

"Are you going to the Sarround Gala?" Romeo lifted his chin to face me directly after sipping his drink.

I sighed, but this time, I didn't roll my eyes at the mention of that black tie event. I knew it was coming up soon, but I hadn't been thinking about it recently. Those gatherings were normally a pain in the ass. Too many players in one place. Too much tension that could boil over at any minute. And all the while, we had to smile and act like nothing was amiss.

"Yes."

"You hate socializing at those things," he commented with a smirk.

I nodded. "Usually, I do." *Not this time.* I was looking forward to that night for the first time in many years. I had just been thinking about wanting another opportunity to take Nina out so I'd have an excuse to kiss her and touch her in public. All to push this idea that we were together. The Sarround Gala was an excellent opportunity for that. "I'll be there. With Nina."

Franco scrolled on his phone, furrowing his brow as he focused on whatever he read, but he still nodded, acknowledging what I said.

"With Nina," Romeo confirmed.

I looked him square in the eye.

"Are you with Nina to throw Vanessa off your tail?" He leaned back in his seat and crossed his arms, looking mighty smug about asking me such a question.

I didn't take bait to his teasing tone. "Since when do you concern yourself with the women I date?"

Franco laughed once without looking up from his phone as he continued to multitask. "Date? You've never dated Vanessa."

And I never, ever fucking will. Even if Stefan hadn't crossed a line in presuming the Giovanni Family could count on an alliance with the Constellas, I was sick of that predatory woman.

"You've never dated anyone. Period," Romeo teased.

I shrugged, declining one second of the pressure to reply on this matter.

"What gives?" Romeo asked. "After the situation I found her in at Escott's, not to mention seeing her sitting on your lap like she'd become your favorite pet…"

I sighed. Pet? That was too damn trivial and cute of a name for the woman I lusted for. I dreamed about her nightly. My random thoughts circled back to her. Nina had crept so close without trying to. She was under my skin and on my mind, and there wasn't much room for me to try to deny it.

"It started out like that," I confessed.

"What did?" Romeo asked. Franco glanced at me for a second, curious as well.

"I started to see Nina to show Vanessa that I'm taken."

Romeo frowned. "She wasn't at the dinner at Escott's that night."

"No," Franco said, "but I think word is spreading about his being there with Nina."

"And after I arrive at the Sarround Gala with her on my arm, everyone will see for themselves that she's with me."

My son was too astute to just take my word for anything. He focused on a few. "What do you mean *you started to see Nina* for that reason?"

I searched for the right words to explain it all. While I wasn't ashamed of admitting that I asked Nina, my friend's daughter, to pretend to be my girlfriend, it now seemed like a lie. Like an inaccuracy.

Nina had come to matter to me, so much in such a short time. I wanted her with a hunger I wasn't sure I could stave off for much longer, so telling my top two trusted men that she was only in my life to pretend we were a couple felt like a sham.

I want her. But I swallowed that honest truth, avoiding telling them here and now.

Nina should be the first person to hear that statement. I wanted to express my desire to her—and act on it.

One question remained. Only one decision was left for me to make.

Should I tell her before or after that gala? Because it no longer seemed like such a good choice to bottle it all in.

Life was too damn short to waste on anything—both good and bad.

If Nina had come into my life to be rescued from a promise to the bikers I refused to work with, maybe she'd rescued me too—from an empty future of utter loneliness.

16

NINA

Nina

The next day, I went back to the gym in the lowest level of the mansion. Before I moved in here, self-care and making my health a priority were a farfetched ideal. I worked too much. I didn't have money for a gym membership or any equipment.

Here, I felt like a spoiled guest to really get into the addiction of cardio. I suspected that I wasn't using the weight machines properly, but so far, I hadn't strained anything.

Running on the treadmill had become my favorite, and it was how Dante found me—again.

Yesterday, he'd caught me when I'd already left the gym. Today, he entered the room and watched me finish my cool down.

I laughed, unable to stop myself. "Are you following me?" I joked. I wasn't sure how he could've guessed that I would be here. Maybe he was following me and I was already that predictable.

"I've noticed you like coming down to the gym." He shrugged, taking his time to look me over as I stopped the machine and stepped off the belt. "I had a hunch you'd be at it again."

"I think I'm getting hooked on it." I wiped my face with a towel, but I was still soaked through. As I headed toward the counter to get my water bottle, I pulled my zipped-up hoodie off and tossed it into the laundry bin in the corner. It was drenched, as were my tank top and pants. Removing those layers would feel so good, but I wasn't ready to reveal that much skin to him.

Just like at the pool, I was nervous to expose myself. It felt too risky.

I drank my water, watching him check me out as I rehydrated.

It was no casual glance. Dante took his time looking me over with an appreciative hunger. His lips, usually so firm with a smirk, curled upward, like he was trying to hide a wide smile.

"Mr. Constella," I chided as I turned toward the door to leave.

He followed me, brows raised. "Hmm?"

Looking back once, I caught him staring at my ass. And it felt good. Having his attention was the reward I'd been hoping for. Ever since that other night when he came to check on me after the dinner, I'd fallen headfirst into this rampant desire. I wanted to impress him. I wished for him to notice me and like what he saw.

Right now, staring unabashedly at my ass and grinning so wickedly, I knew he did.

"No one's here."

He rubbed his jaw, looking up at me. "That's true."

And... you like that?

"Then save"—I spiraled my finger at his face as we walked—"that starved-man look for later."

"Starved man?"

I laughed lightly. "Yeah. Save those kinds of looks for when someone's watching."

"Life is too short to save up anything for later."

His words were cryptic, but not alarmingly so.

"So, if I want to look my fill of your tempting body…" He dropped his gaze to my breasts. As if feeling his stare, my nipples seemed to point out from under the wet fabric even more.

"Fuck, Nina." He stopped me by pushing me against the wall so suddenly that my water bottle fell to the ground. It spilled, splashing out on my shoes, but I was glad he remained dry and fine in his suit.

"Mr.—"

He growled, leaning in closer and slamming his lips to my mouth. Hints of mint and coffee reached my tongue as he took over the kiss. He demanded. He explored. Without any warning, he silenced me fully and triggered me to drown in desire.

Bracing his hands against the wall, he kept me right where he wanted me, in place and dueling with his tongue.

All I could do was try to please him. To keep up with his hunger and kiss back as hard as he did me. To let him in. To enjoy his need to have this forbidden, sensual contact.

I panted hard, breathing harshly through my nose as I moaned under the rough kiss. I was already catching up with my respiration from running and my workout, but Dante had me breathless. Senseless, too. All I felt, all I wanted to experience, was him. The soft firmness of his lips brushing against mine. The wet slide of his tongue along mine.

Arching into him, I showed how badly I wanted this. How desperately I'd been wanting *him*. But I didn't dare touch him. I couldn't.

"Nina…" He said on a rough exhale once he broke for air.

"I thought I was supposed to be Ms. Bardot." As I licked my lips, breathing hard and fast for my racing heart, I stared into the darkness of his brown stare. It was a smoldering look, full of heat and need.

"Consider this practice, then." He leaned in again, fusing his mouth to mine and kissing me even harder. Desire pummeled through me, but I tried not to mess him up.

When he parted again, I furrowed my brow. "Practice? Practice for what?"

He slanted toward me, nipping and gently kissing my lower lip. With a lazy, slow, and leisurely manner, he sampled me, like he had all the time in the world despite the fact that he was dressed and ready to leave, likely for another meeting.

"For tomorrow night," he answered, still kissing me softly. I couldn't resist. Catching his mouth again, I replied in kind.

"What's tomorrow night?" I lifted my hand to rub it over his chest but stopped before I touched him.

"Why are you holding back?"

I curled my hand into a fist and lowered it. "I don't want to get you dirty or sweaty."

He hummed. "Maybe later." Again, I was mute under his lips as he kissed me longer.

"All I want to do is think about being dirty with you," he growled before he licked his lips, no doubt tasting the salt from my lips and skin.

"Mr. Constella," I whispered, shocked and so turned on that I didn't know how I had the energy to get excited after the strenuous run. This was the time to cool down, to slow my body and recoup from the exercise. Instead, I was charging forward with so much thrilling need for him that I struggled to breathe steadily.

"No." He kissed me harder, pushing me into the wall. "Say my name."

My God. I didn't know what was happening, if he was giving up on faking anything and I missed the memo.

"Dante." I moaned under his answering kiss.

"Dante," I tried again. "Practice for what?" It was those little words that kept me from thinking this was real, that he had broken and lost control of the maddening sexual tension sparking between us.

"For tomorrow night. The gala." He just couldn't stop kissing me, taunting me to reach out and hold him close, to push and grind against him before I looped my legs around his waist.

"You'll be there with me," he whispered.

"And… you want to practice how to kiss?" I asked, hating how dumb I sounded.

His chuckle didn't clue me in. It was a low and wicked sound that turned me on more. He oozed such masculinity, such intelligence and confidence, that I could revel in amusing him. Even at the expense of admitting I was asking something stupid. Something obvious.

"Sure. Call this practice for kissing at the gala." He looked down at me, growling at the sight of my nipples so hard beneath the wet fabric. "We'll practice as much as you want."

I felt like we were talking in riddles. Practicing kissing sounded like an excuse to make out with me. But I played along, anyway. "You'll teach me?" I asked as I traced the tip of my tongue along his upper lip until he kissed me. "You'll show me what I need to know? How to look like I'm with you and making you happy?"

"I'll teach you anything you want to know," he replied, his voice so deep and husky, threaded with desire.

He wasn't faking a damn thing right now. Ignoring my whimper of protest as he pushed his body against mine, flush and dirtying his suit with the contact, he kissed me until I thought I'd pass out.

"But I'm not..." I licked my lips and stared up at him, amazed at the lust glittering from his deep brown gaze. "I'm not ready."

"For what, Nina?" He trailed kisses along my jaw, going for my ear and not at all bothered with how sweaty I was. "Ready for *me?*'

Oh, fuck. I prayed that he meant that like I thought he did. Sexually. Intimately.

I swallowed hard, struggling to keep up with this naughty talk. "For the gala."

He smiled roguishly. "Then I'll take you to get something."

Again? "Maybe this time," I said quietly, "*you* can help me pick something suitable."

He kissed me once more. "Absolutely." Then he stepped back, bringing his hands off the wall. "Tonight."

I nodded, too stunned and dizzy with desire to say anything coherent yet. "Okay."

He stared at me, lingering for another heated, torturous moment. With every second that passed, I was tempted to launch into his arms and get right back to kissing the smirk off his lips and earning his sexy, guttural growls of satisfaction and neediness.

"We'll practice some more," he said as he began to back up.

"Practice makes perfect," I quipped, too stupefied from his kisses to say anything wittier.

He shook his head. "You already are."

I bit my lower lip to keep from smiling too widely. It wouldn't do to show him how much his flirty attitude got to me. I had to stay strong.

But why?

As he turned and left me there, slumped against the wall, I felt more confident that he was talking about something else. He wasn't suggesting that we practice kissing and being close for the sake of perfecting our fake relationship that would need to be noticed at this gala tomorrow night. Reading between the lines, I got a strong hunch that he was mocking me, teasing me with the idea of practicing for the real thing.

A real attempt at being together.

I lifted my fingers to my swollen lips, happily abused by his demands for kisses.

And I wondered what would happen the next time he spotted me and insisted that I call him by his name. Because maybe that could be the trick to make him snap and kiss me once more.

Calling him Mr. Constella was a sassy reminder that we were supposed to make our connection believable when others were watching. Referring to him by his name in private like this… That was much more fun, especially when it drove him to want to taste the syllables right off my tongue.

17

DANTE

Dante

I returned to the house in the evening. The excitement to see Nina again kept me distracted all day, but it was my niece who I found finishing dinner in the kitchen, not Nina, as I'd hoped. After that lie about kissing her for practice, my fake girlfriend had consumed my every thought.

Eva kept to herself most of the time, but I knew she'd followed my instruction to help Nina settle in here. Whenever we spoke, she badgered me with questions about her.

Now was no exception.

"Are you going to the Sarround Gala?" she asked after she wiped her mouth.

I nodded.

"With Nina."

It could've been a question but she said it like an affirmation.

"Yes."

She set the napkin down. "Is that smart?"

I paused for longer than I wanted to. I'd already eaten, and I guessed that Nina had too. Nothing should delay me from taking her out to get a dress, something I had been looking forward to all day. Last time, I foisted her onto that sales clerk. This time, I wanted to participate in the selection of her gown. I'd take any and every opportunity to "practice" anything with the woman who was consuming me, body and soul. Something about her just drew me in, and it felt like I was playing with fire to resist her.

"What do you mean?" Eva had been resistant to the idea of having another woman in the house since the first day. Initially, I'd assumed it was a threat to her. That somehow, having another woman challenged her importance here. My niece had always been protective of me and Romeo, and I appreciated it. Loyalty was important in the family, but she took it to another level.

"She was hurt the last time you took her out."

I shook my head, guessing where she was going with this. That parading Nina as my girlfriend would endanger her. "Those servers were not connected to any of our rivals."

"Still." She shrugged and stood. After she put her dish and glass in the sink, she faced me again. "Everyone will be at the gala. Everyone will see you with her."

I nodded. That was the whole point, the purpose of throwing them all off.

"I can't shake the suspicion that she's keeping something from us. From you." Her arms folded over her chest, but her haughty stance wouldn't sway me.

"I applaud you for maintaining a high guard, Eva." I stepped closer to press a kiss to the top of her hair. She was such a ball buster as a child, and she'd grown into a fierce woman—if a little too much sometimes with her attitude. "But Nina isn't up to anything nefarious."

I found her in her room, and I took a moment to appreciate her napping on the lounger near the windows. Like this, she looked so peaceful and content, at ease without any rules about pretending anything or remembering to call me a formal name when no one was around. I preferred her easygoing and relaxed, like she was this morning after her workout. I relished her banter and the ease with which she could meet me in the middle with the desire simmering between us.

Tempted to wake her with my lips, I sighed and willed myself to stay strong. The restraint I had around her was slipping. Too soon, I'd deviate from practicing anything and pretending at all. I wanted her with a stubbornness I couldn't switch off. She was forbidden, delegated as something to fake, not to treasure. Yet, I wanted to, so badly.

"Nina." I sat next to her, and that slight dip on the cushions roused her.

"Oh!" She opened her eyes quickly, jarred from her nap with a hint of embarrassment. As her cheeks turned pink, I held back a groan. Seeing how far that flush could spread from her face was one of my biggest fantasies.

"Sorry. I just dozed and…" As she sat up, the book she must have been reading fell to the floor. It bounced off my shoes, but I couldn't be pulled from staring into her eyes.

She rose to sit in front of me, bringing her face—and those sweet lips—so close to mine. A breath away. An inch apart. So close that all I had to do was bridge this gap and pick up where we left off earlier.

"Mr. Constella," she said quietly, playful and a little unsure. "If you keep looking at me like that…" Her lidded gaze dropped to my lips and she sighed. "We'll never find me a dress."

"Is that so?" I slanted closer, keeping my mouth right by hers. Our breath mingled, and I licked my lips.

She nodded, bumping her nose with mine. "Yeah."

"Then how should I look at you?" I taunted, lifting my hand to cup her face. The first touch of her smooth, soft skin was my undoing. She pulled me to her. I was drawn to her, wanting it all.

She tipped her chin up in an effort to initiate a kiss, but she lowered again as she seemed to think twice.

Suddenly, that was my goal. I'd pursued her every time. I always took the first step. I made the move. With the rules of pretending to date, maybe that was how it should be. But I wanted her to initiate it. I wanted her to act on this magnetism locking us together.

"We should go," she said, rearing back.

Before she could retreat fully, I slid my fingers on the back of her head and kept her close. "How do you *want* me to look at you?"

Breathing quickly, she reacted with some kind of naughty idea. But she wouldn't share it with me.

Slow down. This is too much. I couldn't assume she was an expert at this game of seduction. Because that was what we were playing with here. We weren't pretending anything. We were caught in a layered battle of wills, of trying to stay afloat in this desire.

I compromised, pressing a quick kiss to her cheek. "Let's go." I took her hand and led her to the car, hoping she realized that I wanted to touch her, even with this simple gesture of our fingers entwined, even though no one was watching.

"More practice?" she teased, squeezing my fingers.

"Yes. Brace yourself for more lessons," I warned.

"Lessons about what?" she asked at the car.

"About what it looks like to be my woman."

The ride to the dress store was a quiet one. With the constant thrum of sexual tension and attraction burning between us, it seemed we didn't need to talk. We conveyed our thoughts with little stolen glimpses of each other. Secret smiles and avoiding eye contact. Accidental brushes of our hands as I shifted the sports car.

Once we got there, I told the attendant that I wanted multiple options laid out for Nina in the private fitting suite. Nina raised her brows at me, not expecting my supervision over this dress selection.

"No phone calls tonight?" she asked as the woman measured her to better gauge what to bring out for her.

I shoved my hands in my pockets and raked my stare over her standing on the dais with her arms outstretched. The woman brought the tape measurer length up near Nina's breasts, and my fingers itched to be the one so near her like that there.

"No. No phone calls." *Tonight, I'm all yours.* She seemed to read that in my gaze because she blushed and lowered her gaze.

The shop attendant picked up on the cues that I wanted privacy with Nina as well. She led us to the massive changing area and pointed out the racks that she and her assistant had chosen for us.

"If you need anything, please let me know." With a dip of her chin, she bade us farewell and closed the door behind us.

"Aren't you going to step out?" Nina asked.

I lowered to the chair and hooked my hands behind my head. "Do you want me to?"

She opened and closed her mouth, too intimidated to look me in the eye. After she turned in a slow circle, browsing the dresses instead of facing me directly, she found my reflection in the mirror. "Is this more practice?"

I smirked. "Show me the dresses, Nina."

She bit her lip, teasing me with that telltale show of her nervousness. "All right."

I steadied my breaths as she removed her clothes. This personal, private show was torturous hell. With every inch of her taut, smooth skin that she bared, I fought the urge to get up and claim her.

No longer blushing, but modest to avoid eye contact, she walked over to the first rack and picked up two options. "Blue or green?"

"Neither."

She jerked her face up, surprised and confused.

"I prefer you like that." In a lacy black bra with her breasts almost spilling out, and the tiniest black thong that showcased her perfect ass.

"You want me to go to a black tie event like this?" she teased, falling into the playfulness she saved for me when we were alone.

I shook my head and growled. *I want you dressed like that, and in less, just for me. For my eyes only.*

"How about this?" She held up an inky black dress.

"Try it on."

Watching her slide the clingy material over her hips was just as sexy as watching her take off her shirt and shorts. It suited her. I bet all of them would. This was only the beginning, though, and I intended to get my fill of watching her dress and undress. Each time she changed and then did a twirl to show off the gowns, her eyes grew darker with desire.

Showing herself off like this, putting on a show for me, was turning her on too.

When she struggled with a zipper, I curled my finger and beckoned for her to come to me.

"Did you like that one?" she asked as I dragged the metal tab down. Seated like this, I was at a perfect level to stare at the expanse of her tanned flesh. The slender curve of her back taunted me, and I reached up to push the gown off her.

Touching my fingertips to her caused goosebumps to raise on her skin, but she didn't flinch or step away.

"I like *you*," I replied as the silver garment slithered off her, cascading to the floor. Catching her reflection in the mirror, I spread my hands over her hips, bracing her to stay between my knees.

Her breath hitched as I lowered my hands to rub over the cheeks of her juicy ass.

"I like you looking at me like this," she admitted as she stepped back toward me.

I hummed my approval, taking my time to feel up her almost naked body.

"Do you now?" I tore my focus from her backside and stared into her reflection. As I moved my hand forward, I slipped my fingers beneath the elastic of her thong. Urging her to back into me, I spread my legs wider and pushed on her stomach.

She obeyed, retreating until the backs of her thighs bumped into me. Under the pressure of my hand, she lowered onto my lap, straddling me.

"How about now?" I asked as I kissed up the side of her neck. With her legs splayed apart, she couldn't miss the movement of my fingers stroking along her wet pussy lips.

She nodded, panting as she melted against me. "Yes, Dante. Yes."

"I like it when you say my name like that." I rubbed against her clit, suckling at her neck.

"I'll say whatever you want, as long as you don't stop."

"Not even to do this?" I dipped my fingers lower, pushing them into her tight, wet heat.

"*Oh...*" she moaned, closing her eyes as she rolled her head on my shoulder. "Dante. Please."

Fuck, I liked her begging. I couldn't get enough of her. Those sexy, breathless gasps. The desperation in her grinds down on my lap.

"What about this?" I asked as I brought my hand up over her stomach to her cleavage. One twist of my fingers unclasped her bra. As the satiny fabric dropped to the floor, her tits fell free. Perky nipples pointed at our reflections in the mirror, and I didn't waste time covering her breast with my hand, weighing it, stroking and cupping it. My thumbs flicked over her nipples, and she arched her back.

"Dante. More." She pushed into my hands, both on her breasts and her pussy.

I nipped at her neck and pushed her to stand. "More?"

She stood, staring at us in the mirror. "Please. I want you, Dante."

"Then get these off." I pulled up the band on her thong and let it snap back onto her skin.

While she shimmied out of the now-wet lingerie, I unzipped and lowered my pants and boxers. I didn't leave the chair, pushing up only to shove my clothes down. By the time I had my dick free, jutting up and eager to sink into her, she crawled back toward me. Keeping her legs apart, she lowered to my lap again, rubbing her bare pussy lips along my cock.

"Do you like me looking at you like this?" I asked as I guided her to my dick. She stared at it, lust clear on her face as she nodded. Nothing could pull her gaze away from my glistening dick so near her entrance. Smeared with her cream, I was ready to thrust into her, and I lined her up. My cockhead spread her open, and although I wanted to slam her down on me in one rushed drop, I dragged it out.

She sank down on me slowly, and with every inch of the stretch as I impaled her, she moaned and breathed frantically, overwhelmed with the tension. My dick was so hard it hurt, but I gritted my teeth and avoided rushing it. I wanted to savor every second, every moment of her gloving me so tightly. All the sensations of her small body seated on mine, lax and trusting and so warm to hold.

"Yes, Dante," she replied once she caught her breath.

I was all the way in, and I let her acclimate to the fullness while I cupped her breasts and rubbed and tugged at her nipples. Kissing along her neck, I tasted the essence of her surrender.

"How about this?" I teased, pushing her hips so I could slide out of her, then slam back in.

She cried out, so loud anyone outside this suite could hear. "Yes!"

"Watch us, Nina. Watch how we fit." I urged her to lean forward, resting her hands on my knees. With her slanted forward, she could arch her back and push her ass toward me, meeting me thrust for thrust.

I held her thighs, gripping her legs to force them apart. Her breasts jiggled and swayed. Her pussy clenched around my hardness. And with a few more faster thrusts, I pushed her over the edge.

"That's it. Just like that."

She groaned, trembling and losing her strength to brace herself over me like this. Before she fell, quivering and shaking as her orgasm overwhelmed her, I hugged her back to me and pushed into her sweet pussy three more times. That was all it took to make me lose my load. I flooded her with my hot cum, and with each pulsing jerk, I dug my fingers into her hips and secured her down on my lap with no gap between us.

For several long moments, we sat there united. She lay against me, limp and sated as I rubbed her upper arm and helped her come down from the high of her climax. Eventually, we'd need to get up, to clean off the mess and get out of here. Right now, I was content to stare at our reflections and admire the union of my dick deep inside her.

After all the waiting and denying, all the suspense and resistance we instated between us, we were left without a single word. We didn't need any words, either. We'd fallen, mutually surrendered together to this unshakable need that burned from the instant we ran into each other.

But I finally broke the silence. "Get the black gown," I told her, looking forward to seeing her at the Sarround Gala at my side.

18

NINA

Nina

I smiled at his choice. The long black gown didn't hide much of my boobs, but it wasn't overly provocative like the skimpier dress I'd worn to Escott's. At this gala, we'd be surrounded by more people. I would trust Dante's judgment. I'd trusted him to lead me to pleasure, and he'd exceeded my expectations there.

As he slipped out of me now, I watched a bit of blood smear against my inner thigh.

Most women likely lost their virginity under more modest terms. With the lights off. On a bed. Under the covers.

Not me.

I gave Dante my V card on his lap. With bright lights to better illuminate a garment choice in this fitting room.

"The black one?" I asked, biting back a wide smile. If he could say anything after fucking me senseless, that was the last thing I expected to hear—his pick of what gown to wear tomorrow night.

Right now, I didn't want to wear anything but this loopy, sated smile and the remnants of our cum drying on my skin.

I almost couldn't believe we'd done it. After the last three weeks of resisting each other—in the name of keeping it fake—we both caved.

"Yes." He kissed my shoulder and prompted me to get off his lap.

I did, wincing slightly at the burn of strained muscles. Muscles I hadn't even known I possessed.

"I like that one the best." He stood behind me. With his pants down at his ankles, he grabbed my arms and waited for me to steady myself. "It's the one I looked forward to taking off you the most."

I turned, smirking at him. "You were grading the gowns based on the ease of taking them off after I wore them?"

"Not the ease." He reached for a box of tissues on a small table and handed them to me to help me clean up. "But how much they prompted me to want to get them off." As he wiped himself off then pulled his clothes back on, he shot me a smug look. "Now that I've finally seen all of you, I much prefer you naked." He wrapped his arm around me and lowered his hand to help me clean up. His fingers lay over mine near my entrance, and even that turned me on even though I was still coming down from the high of that orgasm.

"I can't walk around naked," I teased back.

"Of course not." He kissed me slow and sweet, almost tenderly. "Because I don't intend to let anyone else see you like this."

I sighed, overwhelmed by his affectionate words. They were possessive and controlling, but I liked it. He *was* my hero, and I doubted anything could change that.

Except maybe the fact that we're supposed to be faking it all.

"I'll handle the details with the attendant." He looked me over, smiling like he was proud of his conquest with me. On his way toward the door, he picked up the black gown. "You take your time and come out front."

I nodded, glad he was giving me a little space to adjust. I wanted him close. As soon as he left the room, I missed him, but I had to get my head back on straight. I needed the freedom to breathe and think.

After I tugged my clothes back on, I winced at the press of my shorts. I stuffed my damp thong in my pocket. They were slick with my juices from how aroused he'd made me. The stitches of my denim shorts rubbed against my sensitive flesh. While it wasn't painful, it was different.

Before I left the fitting room, I felt a buzz in my pocket. I paused in my step, pulling my phone out to see that Tessa was calling.

I bet Dante wouldn't be upset if I stalled for a moment or two.

"Hello?"

"Hey. You're a hard lady to reach."

I smiled and smoothed my hair away from my face. "How so?"

"I called you. Like, ten times in as many minutes!"

Yikes. "Sorry. I was, um. Busy."

"Yeah? What could've been so important that you didn't answer the phone?"

She wasn't whining. Tessa was too chill to actually be this demanding of me. But the rule of thumb between us was that if we called consecutively more than three times, it was urgent.

"Well…" I dragged my toes over the plush carpet.

"What?" She laughed lightly. "You sound funny."

"Probably because I just had sex with Dante."

"You *what?*" She screeched it, shouting so loudly that I pulled the phone from my ear and winced for a second or two. "You slept with him?"

I scanned the fitting room, glancing at all the discarded dresses. I settled my gaze on the chair Dante sat in to push me to come so hard.

"No sleeping… We were, uh, trying to find a dress for a gala tomorrow, and one thing led to another."

"Nina!" she gasped. "Seriously?"

I bit my lip and nodded even though she couldn't see. "In a fitting room." I didn't know why I whispered. No one could possibly hear me in here. Or if they could, the loud cries and shouts would've given away what we were doing.

"That's wicked, girl."

"I feel so naughty, but it was bound to happen. I mean, just yesterday, he tried to say that we were 'practicing' kissing and—"

"Okay. You can give me the details later."

I furrowed my brow at her abrupt cut off. Then I recalled that she'd contacted me. Ten times with no answer. "Yeah. I can. What's wrong?"

"Everything!" She groaned loudly. "My parents are getting ridiculous."

They always have been ridiculous.

"They keep pressuring me to get onboard with the idea of marrying Elliot."

I cringed, hanging up the dresses on the racks while I listened to her worries. Mr. and Mrs. West had made it clear that they wanted Tessa, their only child, to marry the son of a family friend. If Elliot were a decent man, I supposed Tessa wouldn't be so adamant to avoid the future her parents envisioned for her. But he wasn't. Elliot was a creepy, sleazy, and weird man. For all his faults, he had something the Wests valued greatly—money. Elliot was a successful but likely corrupt lawyer. Tessa had been telling them no, that she wanted to choose someone of her own picking to marry, but they wouldn't listen.

Listening to her rant about how pushy her mom was, encouraging her to contact Elliot more often, then how her father would lecture her almost nightly, I tidied up the fitting room.

She didn't let me get a word in edgewise, but that was fine with me. After I set her call to speaker, I saw that Dante had texted me.

Dante: *Are you all right?*

Nina: *Yeah. Got a call from my friend. She seems to need a moment of girl talk.*

Dante: *So you're the sort of woman to kiss and tell?*

I smirked, twisting my lips at his playfulness. He was such a badass, hardcore Mafia boss all the time. With me, in private, he loosened up.

Nina: *Correct my memory, but I don't recall having the privilege of kissing you very much in this fitting room.*

Dante: *Next time, then.*

Nina: *Next time we share a fitting room?*

It wasn't supposed to be this fun, teasing him. This banter wasn't fake. Neither was riding his dick. I rubbed my face, torn by how far off the path we'd gotten. I wouldn't take a second of it back, but I wanted to know when a "next time" would come.

Dante: *Next time I fill your tight pussy with my dick.*

I pulled my lips in and fought back a grin. *Oh, boy.* I had a hunch this was what he was referring to when he told me to be careful what I wished for. I'd told him to act like he was with me, and he sure was up to that challenge. Deep down, I suspected he hadn't been acting at all today. Not with those so-called practice kisses, nor with the torrid quickie we'd shared in here.

"Nina?"

I jolted at Tessa's sharper use of my name.

"Are you even listening?"

I winced. "I am." *No. Not really.* Dante was so good at derailing me and making me lose my concentration.

"Damn, he really fried a little bit of your brain, huh?"

I smiled, wishing I could laugh along with her joke.

"Was it all that you imagined it could be?" she asked. Like me, she was too busy to ever date much. Tessa was a virgin—unless she was keeping secrets from me.

"No? I'm not sure how to compare it to anything I could've dreamed up." I sighed, almost feeling shy and ashamed about how easily I caved. Dante and I *weren't* in a relationship, or we weren't supposed to be in one. "It just sort of happened."

"And quickly. I mean, yeah, you recognized him as someone you knew a long time ago, but you only ran into him at the Hound and Tea a couple of weeks ago."

"Three weeks," I corrected.

"Which doesn't mean anything bad. Sleeping with a dude on the first date isn't anything to be humiliated about. It's not like I have firsthand expertise on the subject, but casual sex isn't a crime."

I rubbed the back of my neck, feeling the phantom tingle of his lips on it. "It didn't feel casual."

"Hmm. It seems like you're blurring the lines between faking it and falling for your Mafia man."

"The lines are definitely blurred."

"But in a good way, right?" she checked. I could always count on her to worry about me.

"Yes." The slight burn down there, a physical reminder that he'd stretched me, was very good. I wanted him to fill me again. Soon. Just thinking about his touches and carnal looks revved me up to a lusty mess.

"Wow. You replied pretty quickly there."

I smiled. "I guess I'm that confident about how I feel."

"About him? Or about having sex with him?"

Both? "About the sex."

She laughed harder. "One time and you're sold on it?"

I nodded. "Oh, yeah. I'm sold."

She huffed. "Here I am, terrified of marrying someone, and you sound eager to make it official to bang the rest of your life away."

I licked my lips, enjoying this silly talk. I hated that she felt stuck with her situation, but it didn't put a damper on my enthusiasm about Dante now that we'd crossed the lines to have sex. "Yeah. I'd marry Dante in a heartbeat."

Although we laughed together, as I left the fitting room, I realized that while I'd said it in jest, I meant it. One hundred percent.

Dante could very well represent a solid, fulfilling future, but it felt too much like wishful thinking, nonsense to giggle about, than a reality in the making.

I disconnected the call with her and walked out to Dante's car. He leaned against the hood, looking at his phone, and I smiled to myself.

Calling that hunk of a sex god mine—for real—felt like a fantasy.

But the next buzz of my cell in my pocket yanked me away from daydreaming and planted me back in reality.

Ricky: *Nina. You have to come home. Now!*

I furrowed my brow, bothered that this first summons from him came in the form of a demand.

Because he's still expecting to hand me over to those bikers. A car backfired in the parking garage, and its throaty engine resembled the growl of a motorcycle. It was nothing more than a coincidence, this sound reaching my ears right when I had to be reminded of how I was due to go to a dirty MC gang.

I flinched, and just like that, I gave up with this silliness about staying with Dante forever. He'd never said anything about keeping me forever. This was all supposed to be an act, anyway. We'd lapsed, having sex like that, but it really didn't change anything about our arrangement.

He was keeping me close so I could continue to escape a future with the bikers. I still didn't know what his reasons were for wanting to pretend I was his, but as I walked toward him, I wondered if that Vanessa woman stopping over yesterday played a part in his decision.

It's not real, Nina. Remember that. I refused to let the magical afterglow of sex make me stupid.

Too much was at stake for that.

"Ready?" Dante smiled up at me, sensing my approach.

I smiled the best I could, hating that real life was tarnishing the good feelings that filled me after I came with him. "Yeah. I'm ready."

Not.

I wouldn't feel ready until I had an idea of what would be coming at me next.

19

DANTE

Dante

That first day I brought Nina home, I told her that she would need to preoccupy herself. I wanted her to understand that work took precedence and that I was a busy man in demand with my men and associates. At no time was she supposed to be deluded and assume I would play house with her.

And she'd followed that expectation beautifully, spending her time independently, reading, working out, or making herself at home preparing meals in the kitchen.

After I fucked her in the fitting room, she became so aloof that she excelled at staying preoccupied.

It was only one night and one day, but they felt long.

Something happened. Something had to have shifted to make her so distant. She didn't give me the cold shoulder, and she wasn't doling out a silent treatment. But I could tell. I didn't know what it was, but something was bothering her. Ever since I told her that I wanted her to wear that black gown tonight, she had a sense of worry clouding over her.

"All the more reason to look forward to tonight," I whispered to my reflection in the mirror as I adjusted my tie.

If she was shrinking into herself and getting defensive because I took her virginity last night, then I'd set her straight on that behavior. It had to be a big deal to her—having sex for the first time. It was a bigger deal to me, because now that I'd had her, now that I knew how perfect her pussy felt wrapped around my dick, I wanted her again. Even worse than before.

I was her first, and I started to play with the idea of being her last, too.

At the risk of her safety and all.

If Nina became mine for real, she'd need to tolerate the danger of being associated with one of the most notorious crime leaders in the city. That was no small condition to consider or accept.

I checked the time as I left my room, impatient to see Nina in the black gown I chose for her.

Downstairs, I waited until the last possible moment to call her down.

If she's going to be nervous and skittish...

I sighed, bracing to raise my voice and yell for her to hurry. Turning, I lifted my face toward the grand staircase. She was already coming down the steps, carefully holding up her dress as she walked toward me.

"Nina." I didn't yell or scold her to hurry. Her name left my lips in a revered whisper of awe.

"What do you think?" she asked, a little cautious as she glanced at me.

"I like it. A lot." I nodded, holding my hand out for her to take it once she came to the floor. Her grip was steady, but the nervous look in her eyes was not.

"You're gorgeous, Nina." I guided her closer so I could kiss her, but at the last second, she turned her head slightly to avoid my lips.

I tsked after pressing my mouth to her soft cheek and kissing her there. "What's that about?" I growled. Slipping my arm around her back, I tugged her close and hugged her tight. Her faint giggles lifted my spirits. This time, I cupped her face and kissed her sweet lips. Hard and fast. It wasn't enough. I doubted I'd ever get enough of this woman.

"I didn't want you to mess up my makeup."

I kissed her again until she softened and moaned against me.

"I want to mess you up in every dirty way there is," I warned into her ear. Her shivers were my reward, and without releasing her fully, I led her toward the door.

"But first, the gala."

I sighed and nodded. "Yes. First, the gala. Where I can show everyone that you are mine."

We were supposed to only be pretending about it all, but I wondered how I could explain to her that I wanted it to be real between us.

Tonight. The second I bring her home. We left, and as I drove, I envisioned how I'd tell her that things had changed. We'd lie on my bed, naked and tired from fucking hard, and I'd look her in the eyes and tell her that I was done faking anything with her.

Headed to the Sarround Gala wasn't a prime time to realize that I had to update her on what I wanted. But afterward, she'd know the truth.

On the drive there, she asked a variety of questions about the event, and I enjoyed the simpler companionship with her, just talking.

"It's to benefit the children's hospital," I answered after her inquiry about what the gala was a fundraiser for.

"That's altruistic," she quipped.

"It is. But the real reason we go is to keep tabs on our friends and enemies."

"That's a nonstop challenge, though, isn't it?"

I nodded. "It is. And always will be."

"How big of a crowd will be there?"

"At least three hundred?" I guessed. The only comparison I had was my wedding, when I married Grace and had our reception at the same large venue. Five hundred people attended that, and the crowd at last year's Sarround Gala wasn't as well attended as what I remembered from my wedding.

"That's a lot of people." She raised her brows in shock.

I grabbed her hand and kissed her knuckles. "Nothing to be nervous about."

She cleared her throat. "As long as I stick with you, right?"

I chuckled. "Oh, I'm not letting you out of my sight for a second."

The slight increase of pressure on my knuckles soothed me. She wasn't too aloof or nervous to avoid interacting with me.

"This feels like *the* big test. Proving to all the important members of your world that we're an item."

I grinned. *Baby, I think we already are, whether you'll struggle to believe it or not.* "Which shouldn't be too hard to pull off."

She smiled, dipping her chin a bit, almost bashful.

Yeah, you know we're good together. Don't try to deny it.

"Stay with me. Follow my lead," I suggested.

"And play along?"

I can't wait to play with you again.

I had my chance at the gala. We arrived, and I kept my promise. I didn't let her stray more than one inch from me, and I kept her hand in mine the whole time. Or secure in my embrace. Or tucked in against me as we kissed.

She was docile and submissive, truly following my lead. Other women, all decked out in their fine gowns and sporting elaborate makeup and updos, were nothing more than trophies for their partners. Many were likely escorts. Still, we stood out. Nina was a star among the many. Because together, we looked like true partners. A couple. A real pair.

She gazed at me with such trust and open honesty that she would play along with whatever I suggested to her. And she did.

While I stared at her, fantasizing about how I'd peel this shimmering black gown off her gorgeous body tonight, I was aware of how sappy and adoring my expression had to be. If anyone was watching, they'd witness a man very much in lust, and maybe the beginning of love, as I mingled with Nina at my side.

She was no better. After every kiss I stole, following each daring touch, either cupping her ass as I hugged her closer or braced my hand on the back of her neck as I smiled down at her, she looked sated and secure, glad to be with me.

"Mr. Constella," she teased after I handed her another flute of champagne.

I smirked at the formal address. "Yeah?"

"You can't seem to keep your hands off me tonight."

"Try and stop me."

"Who says I want to?" she asked saucily.

The world would see me infatuated with this young woman who impressed me with every turn of this adventure, and I felt like a king, a god, to be able to know she was here for me and with me. Only.

Nina knew how to play her part well, and after I caught a look of surprise on Eva's face as we passed her by, I knew that she had been guessing Nina might not be able to handle the pressure. There was no way to hide or cover up that Nina came from a poorer, deprived background. But no one would know that here. She blended in with the rest of us, elegant, poised, and dressed to impress in that tight black gown that accentuated her curvaceous body.

"Are you enjoying yourself?" I asked her after Franco and I spoke for a while about a few people we were trying to keep an eye on. Stefan was chief among our concerns, but I had yet to spot him in this massive ballroom.

"Yes." She curled up against me, resting her cheek on my chest as she pressed her hand there. "But I wish we could have privacy instead."

"Why?" I asked, eager to know her answer.

She looked me up and down, coy and sexy. "I want you."

I leaned toward her, lowering my hand from the small of her back to hold her ass. Pushing her against me, I whispered into her ear. "You can want me anywhere and everywhere."

I watched her cheek lift in another sly smile. "We couldn't do that here."

"Want to bet?"

Just like that, her expression fell. Gone was the mirthful, teasing nature. She was frowning, focused on something behind me.

Bet? Was that the trigger that bothered her? A reminder that her stupid brother had bet on her life? It was just a saying, and she surely knew that, but I felt so confused as to why she would change her demeanor so quickly.

"Dante."

As soon as *her* voice reached me, I was confident I'd found the reason for the shift in Nina's mood.

Vanessa. Her nasally, whiny tone reached me. Nina curled her fingers into my jacket, and I covered her hand with mine.

"Nina?"

Her brow remained furrowed as she seemed to track Vanessa approaching. I had no doubt that she had locked her determined stare on me, planning to get in my face like she always did. She wouldn't succeed, not while I had Nina in my arms.

"Hmm?" Nina glanced at me a second before I crushed my mouth over hers. Without any further instruction, she played along perfectly. Kissing me back. Moaning slightly. Tilting to ensure a better angle and deeper suction. Her fingers threaded through my hair as she held my head close, and as I wrapped my arms around her, she arched her back to accommodate the force of my kiss, dipping her a bit.

I hoped that coming upon me while I made out with another woman would deter Vanessa completely. Logically, she should've witnessed this display of affection and turned around.

But she didn't. She was still there. Arms crossed and tapping her foot.

"Dante." She repeated it harsher, with more sass and impatience, like I was an asshole to keep her waiting at all.

I sighed, smoothing my thumb over Nina's lower lip that I'd tortured with that hungry kiss.

"Dante." Vanessa wasn't getting the hint.

Nina smirked, and the devilish expression warmed my heart. "I think some lady is trying to speak with you."

"Oh?"

Some lady. I had to fight back a chuckle. Vanessa wouldn't like that label.

"I'm not *some woman*," she snapped as we turned to face her. It was clear that she wouldn't take a hint and leave without saying something.

Keeping Nina pressed against me, my arm around her shoulders, I leaned my head against the top of hers.

"I'm Vanessa Giovanni," she clarified to Nina, her lips curled with disdain.

Nina shrugged one shoulder, indifferent. "Oh."

"She's the daughter of someone I used to know."

Vanessa gaped at me and crossed her arms. "What?"

I didn't back down, maintaining this steady, blank expression. *I said what I said.*

"Used to know?" Vanessa scoffed. "You know my father."

"I used to," I argued. "Lately, it seems he and I have different visions."

Vanessa pursed her lips. "That's not true."

"What does it matter?" Nina tipped her chin up for a kiss, and I obliged her. "He used to know my dad too."

Vanessa's snarl deepened, the best it could with all the work she'd had done. "I don't care who you are. Dante and I—"

I shook my head. "There is no way you can put us together. Not in any claim or sentence you can make up."

"We—"

I sighed, beginning to steer Nina away from her. "There isn't, never was, and never will be a *we* where you are concerned." Pressing another kiss to Nina's temple, I gloated on the victory in Vanessa's glower. She was furious, practically vibrating with how tightly she scowled. If she hadn't gotten the message earlier, she would now.

Mission accomplished.

But the real goal, the real objective, was having Nina at my side.

And I was winning there, too. The reward of Nina's company felt like the ultimate gift I'd ever want in my life.

20

NINA

Nina

Dante led me away from that woman and ended up intercepted by Romeo. He glanced at me, nodding once in acknowledgment, and I appreciated how he didn't act differently, seeing me with his father. I told him that Dante and I were faking this relationship, and he had to be viewing us with that filter of knowledge, knowing we weren't the real deal.

But I was torn with wanting Dante so badly. I was well aware that this was supposed to be fake between us, but I wished otherwise. On his arm, at his side, and receiving his smoldering looks… I felt like I really was his. For as much as he was married to his work, I felt like a solid runner-up. Soaking up his attention was a heady experience. It had me yearning for him and wondering how we could discuss this maybe not being an act.

Once we stepped away from Romeo again, we found a quiet corner. Before I could say a word, he devoured my lips in a hungry kiss that had me questioning what was real and what wasn't. Back here, near the shadows, no one was paying much attention to us. As fervently as he kissed me, though, he was lavishing his utmost focus on me with the goal of complete arousal.

I panted, clinging to him and licking his taste on my lips. Within his embrace, I felt the prod of his erection hardening beneath his pants.

Yes. Please.

"I have to agree with you. I'm enjoying every private moment I can steal with you," he admitted in a gritty, gravelly growl.

I smiled, letting his praise go to my head. Before I could fall into that spiral of lust and let it consume me, I felt like I had to speak up.

"That woman," I began. "Vanessa?"

He sighed, a heavy sound of annoyance. "I don't have anything with her, Nina."

"I'm not sure she knows that."

"She does," he insisted. "I've rejected her nonstop."

"Then maybe she can't accept it." I rubbed my hands up and down his chest. "She stopped by your house the other day."

He frowned, glaring down at me. "What?"

I nodded. "She was a real bitch, knocking on the door and telling me that she was due to have a lunch date with you."

He shook his head, furious, but I put my fingertip to his lips to quiet him. "I knew she was lying. You'd just left. She was pissed when I told her that I was your girlfriend, and she didn't believe me."

"Fuck her. Fucking Vanessa. Don't pay attention to a single thing she says."

"I didn't." I cleared my throat. "I'm sorry I didn't tell you sooner."

He grunted. "I only care if she was bothering you."

I shrugged. "Not really, but you can't blame me for being curious."

He took my hand and led me to a chair in the corner. Back here, away from the bulk of the guests mingling, drinking, and contributing to the silent auctions, we had the relative quiet to really talk. After he sat, he guided me to relax on his lap—which was quickly becoming my favorite spot to be.

"Who is she?" I asked as I smoothed my hand along his firm jaw.

"She's the daughter of one of my former friends," he explained.

"Former? Because he's no longer your friend and is an enemy?" I guessed. Ignorance was still bliss within this Mafia world. I didn't want to know every detail about who was who, and I imagined loyalties and grievances changed often. These Mafia men were killers, prone to responding with violence.

"Stefan Giovanni was my friend way back when. Same with your father. Henry, Stefan, and I ran in the same circles."

I narrowed my eyes. "What? My dad?"

He nodded, stroking his hand up my thigh in a sensual, possessive caress. It almost distracted me, but I was all ears. Dante wasn't just a body to lust after. He was a smart man, a figure from my past, too.

"Yes. Henry drifted apart from me because of his dedication to being in the service. Stefan put distance between us with some of his business choices. Over the years, I didn't agree with a lot that he did with the Giovanni Family, but until now, it's never been a case of declaring him as my enemy. Not publicly declaring him as an enemy."

"What changed that now?" I huffed a weak laugh. "You're upset with him because his daughter is preying on you?"

"She is, though," he said. "She's made it no secret that she wants me. To fuck me. To marry me."

I opened my eyes wide. "Wow." As a waiter walked near, I signaled for him to come closer and let me grab another flute of champagne from his silver tray. After I sipped it, loving the decadence of an expensive alcoholic drink that was a rare luxury for me, I welcomed the warm buzz of the alcohol.

"Needless to say, I do *not* want to mix with the Giovanni Family. Currently or in the future."

"How come?" I asked, trying to think back and do the math on how many drinks I'd had. I followed what Dante told me, but I was definitely well on my way to getting tipsy.

"He allied with another crime organization, the Domino Family. They were unscrupulous, abusive with their power, and determined to monopolize all distribution routes."

I don't wanna know. I don't wanna know. They weren't talking about normal, legal products being transported, but I wasn't going to ask *what* they would argue about.

"Stefan invested a significant amount of money and men into backing the Domino Family, but ultimately, Leo Domino was defeated by the Devil's Brothers."

I blinked, staring at him, stunned. "The same motorcycle club that Ricky lost me in a bet to?"

He nodded, grave and serious about these details.

"Sometimes, it can feel like it's a really small world among us organizational leaders."

I drank faster. "I guess so."

"I want nothing to do with those bikers. They are a newer power in the area, and I am waiting for them to fade from the scene."

Will they, though?

"Do you think that'll happen soon?"

He smiled at me before he brought me close for a tender kiss. "I can't predict that, but rest assured that I will never let them have you."

I liked the sound of that.

"Just the same as your being with me will deter Vanessa from thinking she'll ever have a chance with me."

I froze with his lips pressed against mine. There it was. I finally found the answer. The night we ran into each other at the Hound and Tea, he told me that he had his reasons to want to enter a fake relationship with me. Now I had that reason.

He was using me as a way to show Vanessa that he wasn't available.

And that was the time limit I didn't want to learn. Dante would string me along and keep me near for as long as Vanessa tried to pursue him. Once she found another man to chase, once she gave up on going after Dante, my purpose expire. My ruse would be over. I would no longer have an excuse to sit on his lap or kiss his lips. I would no longer need to enter a fitting room for him to choose a dress for me or bring me close so I could ride his thick cock.

My time with Dante had an end date. And I hated the reminder that this was nothing more than a temporary farce we'd orchestrated.

It's not like it's a surprise. I knew the rules when I entered this arrangement.

That didn't mean I had to like it anymore. Not after we'd both blurred the lines with our very real interest.

I tipped my glass back further, welcoming more alcohol down my throat to numb the pain of not having this rugged, sexy, and powerful man for real.

21

DANTE

Dante

As the night wore on, Nina drank more flutes of champagne. She picked them off the servers' trays more often than what I could count.

"She's probably drinking as much as she can because she can't afford it on her own, right?" Eva asked with more snark than what was necessary.

I faced her slowly, letting her see the disappointment on my face. I'd raised her better than that. She grew up with the expectation of falling in line and behaving like a Mafia princess, but that judgmental bullshit was uncalled for.

She had the grace to lower her gaze and appear ashamed for speaking like that, but she didn't take back her words or apologize.

We spoke off to the side, Eva, Franco, and I, while Romeo and Nina remained a few feet away, looking at an option in the silent auction. I didn't give a shit about any of the choices. I preferred to sink a heavy check with a lot of zeros on it to cover my need to donate to a good cause.

"Or she's just wanting to enjoy the evening," Franco reasoned with Eva.

Nina had seemed like she was having a good time—before Vanessa spoke to us.

Actually, that wasn't true. Nina took that woman's sass and harsh attitude in stride. It was only after, when Nina and I sat down to talk, that Nina's mood changed. While she wasn't aloof like before, she seemed dejected. Defeated. And quickly trying to cover it or numb it with alcohol. I may not have had her in my house for very long, but I was proud of how quickly I'd come to recognize her tells and read her so well.

Regardless of why she wanted to imbibe, she remained as alluring and beautiful as ever. She wasn't a sloppy drunk, but she was sexy, forced to be happier and definitely quicker to be aroused.

She was handsy, all over me, and I loved every fucking second of her sensual attention. Her kisses made me hard. Her lopsided smiles hit me in the heart. And she wasn't on the verge of passing out or tripping over her own feet. She was still in control of herself.

Enough that if I pulled her aside, she would likely unleash all of her desire on me.

And I'd welcome it all.

Through the crowds, I caught a glimpse of Vanessa watching Nina. She had her beaded glare locked on my woman as she spoke with Romeo. Jealousy was evident in her gaze. I didn't like it, and I wasn't sure how long I'd be patient for her to adjust to the visual proof that I was taken. Nina might still think it was supposed to be fake, but she'd know otherwise by the end of the night that what we shared was genuine and ran deeper than lust.

I approached her, eager to revel in the proximity of her warm, soft body at my side again.

"I need to borrow Nina for a moment," I told my son. I directed my comment to him as I took her hand, but I couldn't look away from her smiling, sweet face as I guided her away from the silent auction area.

"Borrow?" Romeo taunted.

"Yeah," Nina joked playfully, twining our fingers together tighter as she followed me. "Borrow me for what?"

"It's typically a saying," I replied as I led her up the stairs. She reached low to bunch up her dress to make her climb easier and smoother. If I were any further in this spell of desire, I'd haul her over my shoulder and spirit her away.

"But right now, I'd like to borrow you for a demonstration."

"Oh?" Her eyes glittered with intoxication and desire.

"Yes. I want you to be my audience."

"Hmm." She looked me up and down. I suffered a unique sense of tunnel vision where she was concerned. When I stared at her, feeling so lucky that we'd ever run into each other like we had, the rest of the world faded away. The chandeliers dripping light down from the vaulted ceilings. The din of hundreds of people speaking over the classical music playing. Nothing registered but the warmth of her hand in mine and her heated gaze on me.

"Your audience to what?" she asked, then licked her lips.

"How badly I want to fuck you."

She smiled wider but trapped her lower lip between her teeth in that telltale way that signaled she was tempted.

"I can only watch?" she teased as we reached the second floor.

I picked up my speed, rushing her along the carpeted corridor. An empty room would be ideal, but this was an ancient recreational and gathering venue, not a residence. I scanned this second floor perimeter, taking in the lack of corners and shadowed alcoves. There had to be a secret spot somewhere up here, but I didn't want to outright run and risk her tripping to keep up.

"No," I replied as curtains swung in a slight breeze. With the summer heat, it made sense that the venue staff would've opened the doors to the balconies lining the upper walls. I led Nina toward one, urging her to step past the navy velvet of the curtains that blocked the narrow balcony space. Underfoot was cement. A carved railing prevented anyone from falling. And as luck would have it, a single small serving table stood out here.

"You're going to help." I spun her toward the table, setting her ass on the surface. After I crushed my lips over hers and rucked up her dress, she caught on to what I had in mind and framed my face. Her sexy mewls and moans made me harder, and as she sucked on my tongue and widened her legs further apart so I could step between them, I knew she wasn't too wasted to figure this out.

The sweet, fruity hints of champagne lingered on her tongue and on her lips. I explored, stealing her taste and demanding that she open up more.

"How…" She panted once I moved my mouth toward her neck. "How can I help?"

"Get my dick out. Right now."

She whimpered as I wrenched the top of her dress low. The fabric ripped a bit, but it was still intact. That black material was now cinched below her breasts, though, shoving them upward so I could suckle and nip at her soft, bare flesh.

"Dante!" She cried out as I sucked hard on one stiff nipple.

"Scream my name. Be my good girl and scream my fucking name."

She whined, frowning at me as the lust seemed to reach a high. Her fingers were slow and clumsy on my zipper, and I thrust into her hand to remind her of what I'd ordered her to do.

"Anyone could hear," she argued weakly.

"Let them all hear."

Her eyes shone from the thrill of what I said. With the soft glow of the lights behind me as I held her on the table out under the night sky, she nodded.

"I want everyone to see what you do to me." I alternated my attention between her breasts. With my tongue, teeth, and lips, I tormented her and wetted her tits until I had to growl at the need to fuck her.

"I want everyone to hear you screaming my fucking name as I pound your pussy."

She succeeded at last, unzipping me and pushing my pants and boxers low enough for my dick to spring out. "You can have me, Dante. Take me." Finishing her bold words that she might not remember later when she was hung over and more sober, she kissed me hard.

I groaned into her mouth as I forced her dress higher. As I shoved my hands up along her soft thighs, she scooted toward the very edge of the table and widened her legs.

"What a waste," I mocked of her panties. It wasn't a thong, but so gauzy and thin that I wondered why she'd bothered. One twist of my fingers on it snapped the bands.

I tucked my arms under her knees, and she gasped as I tilted her back more.

Her hands slammed onto the railing, but she wasn't close to falling over.

"Dante." Her eyes opened wider. At this lower, slanted angle, more light from behind me spilled over her sexy, lusty face. "Anyone could walk by and see."

I grinned, flipping her dress up higher. I wasn't sure I'd agree with her assessment. She was drunker, and at her almost lying flat on the table, she wasn't aware of the curtain that mostly shielded us. Down below, many people walked freely on the sidewalk. Any of them *would* see if they looked up.

"I guess that depends on how loud you are," I teased.

"*Oh*," she moaned as I lined my dick up with her dripping pussy. Rubbing it back and forth, I smeared her juices over her entrance. She was so aroused, so ready to let me in that the slick cream coated my fingers. I switched my hands, spreading her stickiness in quick circles of a rub around her nipples. After I backed up my dick and notched the head of my needy cock at her cunt, I leaned over and licked them clean.

Writhing and squirming, she tried to lock her legs on my arms and pull me into her.

"Delicious, Nina. Such a good girl for me." I slid two fingers into her pussy and brought them up to lick them clean.

Once more, I fingered her and earned her sexy groan. Then I leaned forward to press those wet fingertips to her mouth.

Her lids lowered as I bumped her pussy with my cock again. She opened her mouth and sucked my fingers in, tasting herself. And that was when I slid all the way in until I was seated deep inside her tight heat.

Her moan rumbled over my fingers and hand. The vibration of her hum was paired with her suction, hollowing her cheeks as she tugged my fingers in deeper. I pulled back out to slam in harder. The force of my deep thrust made her tits jiggle, bouncing with every one of my hard pushes into her.

Footsteps sounded behind me. They weren't in sync with the scrapes of the table's legs over the concrete floor. Nina's eyes opened wide as I slowed down my thrusts. Deep inside her, I stayed as still as possible. I maintained the stretch of her hot pussy walls.

I locked my gaze on hers. "Quiet," I ordered softly.

She opened her eyes wider, keeping her lips wrapped around my fingers. Straining to breathe with her mouth full, her nostrils flaring, she looked up at me with shock and nervousness in her tight expression.

"Where did they go?" one man asked behind me.

"I thought I saw them come up here somewhere," another guy replied.

If they were looking for me and Nina, all they had to do was pull the curtain further aside.

I didn't recognize their voices. With my dick deep in Nina, my fingers jammed into her mouth, I strained to listen to what they would say.

22

NINA

Nina

I froze, breathing as hard as I could as Dante stood there. His cock was in me, deep and filling me with that glorious yet trying stretch. With his fingers in my mouth, I was silenced. I could've pushed them out, but I didn't want to protest and risk making a single sound.

His gaze remained on me, daring me to be quiet and still as the men stood right behind him. They stopped in the hallway, and save for a curtain that swayed in the wind, they were oblivious to where we were and what we were doing.

I wasn't doing a damn thing. I was too scared, trapped on Dante's erection and muted with his fingers.

I was drunk, but I wasn't so wasted that I couldn't keep up with the change of events. Sobering quickly to the very real and present danger of being caught with my dress shoved up and my breasts hanging out, I was too nervous to even breathe loudly.

"Are you sure?" the man with the Brooklyn accent asked.

"Yeah, yeah." His partner had a deeper, yet whinier voice. "I know they came up here."

"Romeo's still downstairs," Brooklyn said.

Romeo? Why'd they mention his name?

"And Franco, too," the second man said. "But I swear to God Dante ran up here."

Dante narrowed his eyes, watching me as he listened. His fingers slipped out of my mouth slowly, and with the exit, he pushed my tongue down until he released me completely. I licked my lips, beholden to staring right back up at him.

"Was the woman with him?" Brooklyn asked. "She's been glued to his side all night. I guess it makes sense that she'd go wherever he went."

I gaped at Dante, stunned and terrified that they *were* talking about us. That they were talking about *me*. I didn't belong here. I was the odd woman out. I was the stranger amongst the Mafia regulars who were all familiar with each other. I didn't fit in, and I didn't understand why or how they'd target me.

Because I was seen with Dante? But it's all supposed to be a damn act!

Dante tilted his head to the side, narrowing his eyes as he watched me basically freak out.

"Yeah, that bitch ran up here with him," the second man replied.

I nearly gasped out loud, frightened with this confirmation of men seeking me out. Pressing my hand to my mouth, I muffled any sound. The last thing I wanted to do was give away our location. But as I lay there, stuck on Dante's dick, I was enveloped in complete terror. Tears burned in my eyes as I considered the threat creeping up on me. All I wanted to do was survive, and I'd done so by getting away from Ricky and the bikers who wanted to take me to Reaper. Now, I felt like I was back to square one, facing *more* danger, just for being near Dante.

I couldn't win, and the crushing, overwhelming defeat stung.

Dante shook his head, sensing that I was close to crying, sniffling, or making a noise. Keeping one hand on my hip, he dragged his thick length out of me.

I locked down on the sensations, confused and shocked that he'd... that he'd keep going! Those men were mere feet away, talking about chasing after us, and it couldn't be for any peaceful or amicable reasons. And he wanted to continue fucking me?

I widened my eyes at him, trying to convey that he shouldn't.

He lifted his finger to his closed lips in the universal gesture to be silent. Then he lowered his hand to my other hip. As his fingers dug into my skin, he slowly and steadily thrust back into me.

It was too much. He was so thick, so long, and with an extra shove upward, he gave my clit friction that drove me insane. I swallowed down a moan of pleasure, stuck on him and wanting more. Despite the need to be quiet, I needed more. I yearned for all he'd give me.

It felt too good. Too right. And as he slowly slid in and out, taking his time at an agonizingly slow pace, I closed my eyes and tried to withstand the slow buildup toward an orgasm.

"We're going to have to hang out up here until one of them shows," Brooklyn said, complaining about their fate.

I opened my eyes, alarmed. Dante hardened his face into a more serious expression of determination and moved his hand over. His finger rubbed around my clit, stimulating that bunch of nerves, and I bit down hard on my lower lip to remain silent.

It was torture. Exquisite, perfect torture to be captive under this man's wickedly steady but unrushed touch. I wanted to grip his forearms and urge him to rock into me hard and fast again, making the table's legs scrape on the smooth floor. I debated how dangerous it would be to lead his hands to my breasts and show him how I wanted his touch and caress there.

The second guy in the hallway groaned. "I know. We can't fail. We got our orders, and there's no room for any mistakes."

"If we don't bring that Nina bitch in, if we can't kidnap her, we're fucked."

My mouth hung open. Fear spliced me, severing the ties to the desire Dante encouraged me to savor and experience like this. So taboo and wrong.

At the mention of someone wanting to kidnap me, my blood turned cold. My heart raced faster, and the instinct of fight or flight kicked in with a rush of adrenaline.

Dante shook his head and repositioned his hands. He shoved three fingers of his left hand into my mouth, but he used his right hand to grab my breast, hard. As he pistoned his dick roughly but slowly into me, he pumped his fingers into my mouth. It was his fingers on my nipples that really brought me back to focus.

He wanted me to focus on him. I understood it. He was trying to distract me from the danger within the conversation being held right behind him, and it worked. Mercilessly, he filled my mouth and pounded into my cunt. With the bonus of his fingers on my aching nipple, I knew I wouldn't last.

Before I could come, so close to the pending explosion and release of all that pent-up tension, the second guy's voice filtered through the haze of desire that Dante instilled in me.

"Vanessa needs her out of the way so she can have Constella like she wants."

No!

Dante scowled, focusing on me as he rocked his hips to fill me over and over. At that man's claim, though, he tugged at my nipple so hard, it lent me the right dose of pain that rippled into sweet pleasure.

"Fuck. We can't just stand around here," Brooklyn complained. "Let's walk around this level and then check up on the other side of the building."

"Yeah. Good idea."

Their footsteps faded the further they went, but I hardly heard them to begin with. The roar of my pulse in my ears drowned out everything else. With my heart thundering so fast, beating wildly within my ribs as I strained to breathe quickly enough, I narrowed my eyes with a desperate plea to come.

He nodded, frowning with the strain to fuck me so hard. Even though the threat of those men hearing us or finding us was gone, I was still so close that I was a goner.

Keeping my nipple between his thumb and finger, he slammed into me quickly, and it was all that I needed to go over the edge. I came, sucking and almost choking on the pressure of his fingers in my mouth. Bursting apart from the pressure as warm bliss coasted through me, I arched my back and trembled with the force of my orgasm.

Another quick whip of his hips secured him deep inside me. He came, jerking and spilling his cum in me. While he didn't remove his fingers, from my mouth or my breast, he heaved great, big breaths without making a noise.

Unlike the night before, when we slumped together in that chair, he hung his head and steadied his stance as he caught his breath. My thighs quivered as I let my legs drape lower, off the edge of the table, and he staggered back as he righted his posture.

One quick look back around the curtain must have given him the impression that no one was near. He helped me to sit up, kissing me on the lips as I rose.

"Here." He led me to sit fully upright as I shoved and pulled at my dress to cover my breasts again. My lungs were still working overtime from that rush, but I tried to stay as quiet as possible, anyway.

At the same time that he tugged his clothes back in place, he looked down at my pussy, still exposed, with my legs wide apart and my dress bunched up.

"Dante." I licked my lips and felt the ache in my jaw from his forcing his fingers into my mouth. It felt different, but I hadn't found it unfavorable. "You didn't use a condom."

He shrugged, fixing his clothes still as he stared at my entrance. Warm cum leaked out, and I wanted to push my legs together at the sensation on my sensitive flesh there.

"You didn't use protection last night, either." The slide of our combined juices was a stark reminder of how we hadn't taken any logical precautions.

"I'm clean." He lowered his hands as he glanced at me. "You were a virgin, so you're clean too."

I shook my head. "But I'm not on birth control."

He grinned. "Good."

I gawked at him. "*Good?*" I hissed as softly as I could.

"Yeah." He brought his fingers toward my pussy and pushed the cum right back inside me. I flinched at his touch, so sensitive and overreactive.

"Good," he said. He was unbothered, trying to keep his semen inside me.

Almost like he...

"You'd be happy if you knocked me up?" It sounded crazy once I heard the words out of my mouth, but I needed to hear it from him.

He smirked and nodded. "Yeah, then we wouldn't have to pretend a single fucking thing anymore. You'd be mine, Nina."

He couldn't have surprised me any more than with those severe words. I'd been hoping and fantasizing that I wasn't the only one wanting something real. I'd stooped to silliness and daydreaming about marrying him. If he could admit wanting to impregnate me, like it was the most natural thing in the world...

"Is that what you want?" I asked him, nervous to be so direct and request that he reveal his true intentions. "Do you want—"

A series of gunshots filled the air. It cut me off as I sucked in a quick breath and braced for impact. Sliding off the table, I crashed into him. He caught me, also lowering in a defensive stance. His arms wrapped around me as he kept me plastered to his chest.

Then again, more gunfire followed. Men shouted. Others replied. And then more—and heavier—gunfire.

"Let's get out of here," Dante said. He lifted his head to see over me and scanned left and right down the hallway inside the ballroom.

I was no expert in how far the speed of sound traveled from a source, but I could've sworn it sounded like the fighting and mayhem were happening downstairs. Below us.

Dante didn't hesitate to pull me past the curtain with him, reentering the venue hall. No one aimed a weapon at us in the hallway, so I felt certain the true danger wasn't upon us.

Grabbing his gun from his holster strapped to his side, Dante looked at me with a stern expression. As he held his firearm at the ready, he took my hand with his free one and set off running, sprinting to get us to safety.

23

DANTE

Dante

Nina stayed with me as we ran down the hall. It seemed counterintuitive to rush *toward* the gunfire erupting on the main floor, but it had already died down.

There was no way one group could enter and take out all the guests here. Too many celebrities and politicians had guards and security details. Of the criminal organizations present here, numerous soldiers and men stood on the ready to defend their leaders and capos inside the ballroom.

As I ran down the stairs, I guessed it was a case of two rivals snapping and attacking among the civilians. It happened, but every time we erred and caused too many uninvolved and innocent casualties, it seemed that *all* the crime families were accused and put under an even closer scrutiny with the law enforcement.

"Who is it? Who opened fire?" I shouted at Romeo as he ran up the steps to intercept me dashing down them. Franco hurried Eva off to the side, but several Constella men were surrounding us. All through the commotion of the massive ballroom, leaders were being encircled and protected. Guns were up. Eyes were open. But I saw no easy target to aim at.

Nina remained close to me, her slender fingers tight in my hand. As long as I felt this connection, knowing she was with me, I could stay levelheaded.

"I don't know. Gunfire came in from the side entrance," Romeo called back, frowning as he checked that Nina was all right with me.

I'd never given a shit about coincidences. Someone breaking into this gala *now*, this time, when the event had been put on for many years, meant something.

Nina.

If we hadn't just overheard those two men talking about wanting to kidnap her so I'd be free for Vanessa to claim, I wouldn't have gone there. I wouldn't have jumped immediately to that conclusion. But we had. Moments ago, as I fucked her to distract her from the horror of eavesdropping on a pair of men talking about taking her, those two guys had discussed it.

Is it a diversion? Fighting so they can take her from me? Anger pounded through my veins at the concept. If anyone dared to get in my way and steal Nina from my grasp, there would be no end to the wrath they would incite.

"Is it—" More gunfire cut me off, and I ducked and shielded Nina. She shook beneath me, but the shooting didn't last long.

"What the fuck do you think you're doing here?" Romeo demanded.

I leaned up, glancing over Nina. Down below, past the remaining six or seven stairs I had yet to descend with Nina, was a pair of men. My son was right. They didn't belong here.

Mafia families—the main criminal presence gathered here tonight—did not consort with bikers. The last time a Mafia family attempted to face off with a motorcycle gang was when the Domino Family took them on.

Which was why seeing the members of the Devil's Brothers MC striding in here, guns blazing, made no sense.

"Get the fuck out of here," I ordered, standing tall and aiming my gun at them. Others tried to get through the crowded hall, but with the commotion that the gunfire had caused, people were fleeing and panicking, and there was no easy way to cut through the throngs. Behind the bikers was utter chaos, but these fuckers weren't bothered in the slightest.

"I don't think so," Stefan Giovanni said as he approached. He walked up closer, coming from behind the pair of leather-sporting bikers. One was bald. The other had long, graying, and greasy hair. But both looked like immature idiots with those black and white bandanas tied on their heads.

"What's going on?" Romeo asked as Stefan placed one foot on the first step up the staircase my son and I blocked Nina on. Soldiers filed in, all aiming their guns at Stefan and the two bikers he'd rounded up to face me.

"What's going on?" Stefan laughed dryly at Romeo as more bikers fought security closer to the doors. "I'll tell you what's going on. The joke is up, Dante." He sneered at me, then lowered his stare to Nina. "You've intercepted and had your fun. It's time to hand the girl over."

Nina plastered herself to my back, trembling and tucking in close.

"That woman belongs to Reaper," Stefan insisted.

"The hell she does. According to who? You?" I kept my gun trained on the greasy biker since Stefan wasn't pulling his gun on me. *Yet.*

He canted his head to the left, as though I'd said something ridiculous. "According to the fine, upstanding men in this MC."

Romeo cursed, mocking Stefan's assessment of the bikers' club.

"And Ricky." Stefan narrowed his eyes. "You remember Henry's son, don't you?" Leaning toward the side, he tried to look at Nina crouched behind me. "It looks like you've been really busy making your acquaintance with his daughter."

I didn't respond, letting the asshole squirm under the pressure of my quiet.

He rolled his eyes. "He lost her in a bet—fair and square."

"How the fuck would you know?" Romeo asked.

Stefan shrugged. "I heard about it at the gambling rooms. You know how word spreads and all."

"She's not going anywhere," I told him.

"Oh, but that's just what I promised my new friends." Stefan pushed his hands into his pockets and rocked on his heels. It was a stupid maneuver, and I knew why he was doing it. To look casual and non-threatening. Too bad. I would never, ever lower my guard around my former friend from so long ago. He wouldn't dupe me. Not after he spread word that he could always count on me to back him and align with him when it wasn't true. Nor after his daughter's pushiness to claim me as her husband. And especially not after he sided with the Domino idiots.

"Friends?" I mocked, emphasizing the aim of my gun at the biker. "What, you couldn't beat them with the help of the Dominos, so you're going to join them?"

"I like to stand with power, Dante."

It was a dig, an implication that because I wanted nothing to do with him, I lacked power. *What a joke.* "And they represent power?" I mocked.

"Yeah. Once I heard about how you'd taken Reaper's new lady, I figured I could help them get a little closer so he could claim what he'd been promised."

"Oh." I grunted. "And in exchange, they'd let you in on a deal or two with the regional gun routes? Milk the pot and set up a supposedly mutually beneficial partnership?"

"Don't tell me that you're jealous of me for diversifying." He smiled, smug. "After all, I reached out to *you* first. I tried to get *your* support with those gun routes."

"You didn't reach out to ask for my flexibility or willingness to side with you on anything. You assumed it—incorrectly. Just like you are now in thinking you can invite these stupid fucking bikers in here and do a favor for them."

"That bitch isn't not yours," the bald biker said. "She belongs to Reaper now."

"The hell she does." I firmed my grip on her hand. "She's not going anywhere with you."

"It's time to give her to whom she belongs," Stefan said. "The Devil's Brothers are merely collecting."

I shook my head. "No."

"You've had your fun," Stefan repeated. "But she's not who you're going to partner with or marry."

Hearing that argument from *him*, of all people, irked me to no end. He intended to have me choose his daughter and further secure a connection between the Giovanni and Constella names.

"Not happening." I gritted my teeth and shook my head again. "It's not happening. Nothing will ever happen between me and Vanessa. I will never want your spineless, selfish daughter."

"Watch what you say," he warned. His threat didn't hold much punch, though. As I stepped down, bracing to lunge at him and beat the shit out of him, he staggered back, almost bumping into the bikers.

"No. *You* watch what I say. Listen to me. For the last fucking time, I do not want anything to do with Vanessa." Leveling my glare on him, I raised my voice to be heard over the fighting happening further in the room. "Or you."

Stefan shook his head. "You don't know what you're talking about."

"You're trying to fucking gaslight him?" Romeo scoffed. "Get the fuck out of here. Take your new friends with you, and get the fuck out."

Stefan didn't move, but the bikers reacted. The bald one started talking shit with him, spewing stupid nonsense that left little impact on my son. The greasy guy didn't move his attention away from me. At least he had the common sense to wise up with a gun aimed his way.

"You're not welcome here," I told my former friend. Romeo and I were a unified front here. Father and son. Boss and second-in-command. Together, we represented the mightiest power of the criminal world, and whoever had paused long enough to witness this standoff would see it. They'd recognize the significance of what was happening here.

I'd already refuted Stefan's claims that the Constellas would always back and stand with the Giovannis. Here, in live action, I was showing the world that we never would.

"Don't dare to concern yourself with what I do. Ever again." Reaching back, I took Nina's hand. I felt the tremble in her grip, but she maintained a tight hold. She wasn't weak. Scared, but not so vulnerable that she was reduced to a crying, hysterical mess.

I watched as Stefan turned slightly, addressing the older biker. He spoke too quietly for me to hear what he said, but the thunderous expression on his aging face conveyed enough.

He was livid. Cornered. And pissed that I'd pushed him to admit defeat. He was a moron to risk bringing the Devil's Brothers bikers in here just to try to get Nina out of my protection. He was even stupider yet to align with the MC and count on them for getting ahead.

Holding Nina's hand, I waited for the fucker to turn tail and retreat. He did, and I was content to let the rest of the guests here deal with his invasion. I wasn't the only leader who was bothered with his bringing those assholes to this place, where we were all gathered. And as he tried to exit with his biker friends, multiple soldiers and capos targeted them on their way out, demanding an explanation and warning the MC men to never cross their paths again.

"Dante?"

I hated the fear in Nina's voice as she pulled slightly on my hand, ripping my concentration from watching Stefan leave.

Turning to her, I resolved to erase that tight expression of anxiety from her gorgeous face. Her features should never be taut and strained with such worry, and I despised that she was ever put in this position at all.

"Can we go?" she asked. Her throat tightened with the difficulty of her swallow, more evidence of how tense she was.

"Yes." I exhaled, wishing one simple breath out could purge the tension and rage bottling up inside me. "Let's go home."

She nodded, grateful and clearly at ease that I wouldn't force her to stay here any longer. After the way the MC and Stefan had made their arrival known, with gunfire and anger, I doubted the gala would finish.

Romeo approached us, and Franco wasn't too far behind him. Eva remained off to the side, speaking with the soldiers who stayed with her for security.

"I'm taking her home," I told my son.

He nodded once. Franco did as well before he said, "I've asked more men to follow them out." He narrowed his eyes, seething as he gazed in the direction of where Stefan led the bikers away. "We already knew those assholes were going to cause us trouble."

Romeo smirked. "Sooner than later."

"I'm sorry—"

I tugged Nina to my side, hugging her tighter and silencing her. "None of this is your fault. None of it." Once she lifted her troubled gaze up to meet mine, she frowned.

"I don't want to hear another goddamn word of an apology from your lips," I scolded.

She pressed her mouth shut in a firm line. I couldn't tell if it was stubbornness that had her peeved that I was controlling her like this or that she was refraining from speaking up again.

We had to talk. She had to listen. But not here. As soon as we had some privacy again, we'd discuss it all. Before we arrived, I planned to tell her that I wanted her for good. Now, it seemed I would need to reiterate that, anyway.

Because no one was taking her from me.

Not the Devil's Brothers MC. Not Stefan. No one.

Nina would be mine for good.

24

NINA

Nina

Dante was on the phone on the drive back to his house. From what I could tell as I sat in the passenger seat and let the scenery out the window blur past me, he was checking in with many members of the Constella force. Stefan and those bikers had caused a huge uproar, and I had no doubt that follow-up would be needed.

"You can just drop me off," I said when he wasn't actively on a call. "If you're needed to… do damage control and supervise…"

He shook his head. "No. Romeo and Franco can handle things for me."

"But you don't need to coddle me."

Shooting me a stern look, he urged me to give up that argument. Maybe *coddling* wasn't something a rough, tough man like him could do. "I don't need special treatment."

He didn't reply, answering his phone yet again.

My warm, fuzzy feeling of intoxication was gone. I'd sobered up quickly with Dante's demand to have sex the way we did, so riskily. I'd sobered up even more when I overheard men talking about kidnapping me. Seeing and hearing the gunfire and argument that Dante had with Stefan... well, that knocked me clear out of a buzz and right back into stone-cold reality.

It was a lot to take in. My brain felt too full. I had to compartmentalize all that happened, rationalize my way through all the big emotions. And then, I could feel sane and more like myself again.

Dante wasn't ready to give me time or space to let anything sink in. Instead of leading me to the guest room I'd been staying in, he brought me to his private quarters. *His* room. I didn't give myself a chance to look at the surroundings or slow down to appreciate the dark wood theme that centralized in his sanctuary.

He wanted to keep me close. That was evident in his rejection of Franco driving me home for him. I got the sense that Dante didn't want me out of his sight at all after the gala. He kept my hand firmly in his, which I appreciated because it grounded me. He also refused to go to speak with his men and soldiers, prioritizing my presence.

And here, in his room for the first time, I felt like he wanted to trap me with him.

"I don't need to be supervised," I said as he set his jacket on a chair.

He lined his brow, watching me stand still near the door, too afraid to set another foot forward. "You're not."

I wasn't making myself clear. After licking my lips and hurrying to figure out a better way to word it, I said, "I'm not some delicate weakling." Lifting my chin bolstered my confidence. "I understand that you might perceive me as some young thing to shelter and protect, but I get it, Dante. If you have responsibilities to see to, I don't need you to hover and keep a close eye on me."

He huffed, striding toward me as he unbuttoned his shirt. The slow reveal of his taut, hairy chest stole my attention, and I frowned with how easily he could distract me.

"I don't intend to hover." He dropped his shirt a few feet before reaching me. "But I do want to keep a close eye on you."

Before I could register his intention, he gripped the top of my dress and shoved it down. My breasts popped out, free and unrestrained. Yet, he maintained direct eye contact with me, proving his statement.

"I want to keep a close eye on you tonight." He pushed my dress lower, stretching it as it reached my waist. "Tomorrow." He leaned closer to shove my dress off completely. "And every day after that."

I steadied my breath, overwhelmed by what he said. Without his gaze raking over me, he gave the impression that he wasn't after sex. Not right now. He stared right back at me, confusing me as he removed his pants and boxers. We stood there, naked together, but I realized he was interested in a different kind of intimacy.

He hugged me close, and the flush contact of his hard body against mine felt so familiar and right. I closed my eyes as he kissed the top of my head.

"You intend to keep me?" I asked, thinking back to how defiantly and seriously he told the bikers and Stefan that he wouldn't hand me over. Regardless of the fact that Ricky lost me in a bet. He didn't want to, it seemed, but I wasn't sure how to decipher that.

"I want you with me," he said as he led me toward the bathroom. His fingers locked with mine, and I relished in how comforting his hold was.

"You don't have to pretend here," I reminded him.

"I'm not." He shot me a serious look as he paused at the shower and turned the dual showerheads on. Steam lifted and filled the air quickly, and I shivered, both from the teasing warmth on my skin and the severity of his gaze.

I stepped under the water with him, distracted by his dick jutting out. He didn't initiate anything sexual. After how roughly he took me on the balcony, I was curious about getting more, but I was intrigued about why he'd try to ignore his obvious arousal.

Instead, he hugged me close and began to shower with me. Water sluiced over his chest, heightening the rises and dips of his muscles. Callused and strong—but gentle—he lathered me up and rinsed me off. It was an intimate but peaceful experience that we shared, and I would never forget the tender consideration he showed me.

I didn't speak. I couldn't. I was still trying to figure out what he meant. He wanted to keep me as a permanent placeholder, to make sure Vanessa didn't bother him? Or did he plan to make this real between us?

Accepting this need to think and avoid speaking, I followed his lead. Once I was clean, I tended to him. Soaping him up was just another way to feel his rugged physique, but he broke his control as I did so.

Kissing me slowly and softly, he showed me how much he wanted me. Not only as a pussy to fuck, but a woman to be affectionate with.

After I rinsed him off, we exited the shower together. I stood still, smiling sleepily as he dried me off with a thick, fluffy towel. Tucking the edge of the bath sheet against my breasts, he sighed and stepped back. He grabbed a towel for himself and tipped his chin to indicate that I should leave the bathroom with him.

"Sore?"

I wasn't sure how I could blush around him after he'd already seen all of me. I settled on a shrug. "Not terribly…"

He chuckled, watching me approach the bed. Finished with drying off, he tossed his towel aside and pulled back the covers. I didn't need him to tell me to get in. I could follow a cue. I lowered my towel and crawled onto the mattress, excited and happy that he got in with me.

"I'm not pretending," he told me once we were nestled together. On our sides, we gazed at each other. He picked up a remote and shut the lights off. My eyes adjusted quickly, and I fell in love with the quiet, simple comfort of lying with him and gazing into his eyes. He lifted his hand to stroke my cheek, brushing my hair back from my face.

"What does that mean?"

One side of his lips rose in the start of a sexy smirk. "Are you pretending anymore?"

I shook my head, then turned to kiss his palm as he framed my face. "I struggled to fake it from the beginning."

Now he smiled fully, a self-satisfied, smug expression I wanted to see every day.

"But what does this mean?" I had to know. There was plenty I could assume, but I was too nervous to think he could be true, that he wasn't too good to be true.

"You tell me. If we're not pretending to date, then it's real. We're together—period. What do you want in a relationship with me?"

I raised my brows, thrilled that he was basically giving me a chance to voice my dreams. My fantasies could become reality, and that was a hell of a change to accept.

"What do you want out of your future?" he asked, tucking in closer.

"In general?" I asked.

He nodded, rubbing my back with this tighter embrace. The only distance remaining between us were the few inches so we could face each other for this conversation, but from chest down, we were plastered against each other, cocooned under the sheets and blanket with warmth.

"I've always wanted to go to college." I felt sheepish to say that, since he was so much older and that was not something he could personally relate to. He'd already grown up past the academic years of youth, already had a career, multiple businesses, and great wealth. Every difference between us seemed like another reason we didn't make sense, but I did my best to ignore that.

"For what?" He sounded intrigued, not peeved or irritated that I'd want something so far beneath his age.

"Children's literacy. I've looked into education programs, but I don't want to be a teacher in a classic sense, standing at the front of a classroom. I want to specialize in literacy, though."

He kissed my forehead. "Something simple and good." Then he chuckled. "I like that. It's an ideal opposite to the complicated darkness that I deal with in my life."

"I never had much of a chance to plan for college, let alone work toward it. Ricky took everything, and once Dad died and gave us money in his will, that idiot lost all that too."

He exhaled a long, tired breath. "Henry wasn't around to raise your brother any better."

I nodded, hating that it was true. "And my grandma gave up. She provided shelter and the necessities the best she could, but she'd already raised a child. She already went through parenting and was too tired and unhealthy to want to embrace it again."

"I'm sorry you suffered through your childhood."

"It is what it is. For a long time, I hated that Dad couldn't stay. He abandoned us. But I guess parenthood isn't for everyone. I mean, my mom ran off sooner."

"I think Alison probably realized what a military household looked like and wasn't interested. That's no excuse, but like you claim, it is what it is."

None of us could change the past. I'd dismissed my mother long ago, never having the chance to know her or to remember her. Thinking about the time behind us, I wondered again how my dad, Dante, and Stefan could have ever been friends. More so, that they weren't friends now or hadn't been recently.

"Do you say that in terms of how you all drifted apart? You, my dad, and Stefan?"

"Yes. It's like I told you earlier. We simply wanted different things. We weren't pulled in the same direction." He frowned. "Well, Stefan and I were. We both followed the expectations to take over our families. He became the head of the Giovanni name and I took over the Constella Family when my father died."

"But you are rivals now." I rubbed along his jaw, hoping he could see the gratitude in my eyes. "I appreciate your standing up to him—where I'm concerned."

"Even if he hadn't befriended those bikers, I would've said the same. No one is taking you from me, Nina. I mean it."

Touched by his fierce words, I kissed him, pouring all my love into the press of my lips to his.

"Stefan has made himself my enemy, though. Not only in butting into my life and trying to get me to give you up, but also by siding with those bikers. He sided with the Domino Family before the MC tore them apart, and it's just the most recent things in his pattern of making greedy and stupid choices."

"Is that why Stefan is so eager for you to marry Vanessa? To link you to him somehow?" These Mafia politics would take a long time to figure out. "He seems so certain that you should be with her. Like… like an arranged marriage."

He sighed. "Arranged marriages do happen in our world. It's a common practice for combining Families and strengthening power. I was arranged to marry Grace, and she didn't live two months after

Romeo's birth. Since I'm older, I would hope I could be exempt from that whole ordeal." He smiled. "And since I've found you, I want *you*, no one else."

My heart swelled with hope and love. It seemed far too soon to use the L-word with Dante.

"I'm too powerful as the established boss of the family to be tugged and manipulated into an arranged marriage."

"But did Stefan ever think you had an old agreement or something? Did you talk about the future among the three of you that he'd get so hooked on the possibility of Vanessa marrying you?"

He shook his head. "No. Nothing like that. We didn't talk about that back then." With a wicked grin, he lowered his hand to my ass and pulled me closer to his naked body. "I imagine if Henry were alive and knew what I wanted to do to you, he'd kick my ass."

I bit my lip, properly teased and giddy about Dante's fantasies that might star me. "Oh, yeah? What do you want to do to me?"

The kiss he gave me was slow and seductive. "I'll show you."

25

DANTE

Dante

Other than kissing and holding Nina until we fell asleep, I didn't show her anything. I had many ideas of what I'd like to do with her. To her. But we were both so exhausted and sleepy after that shower that neither of us stayed up late.

When I woke, marveling in the gift of this woman's submission and agreement to stay the night in my bed with me, I lay there and relaxed in the quiet of the morning.

Her routine seemed to be getting up for a quick breakfast and coffee, then working out. It was already past the hour she was usually at it in the gym, so I felt confident that I was spoiling her to sleep in. With me.

It was right where I wanted her every morning, and after our talk last night, I was hopeful that she'd understand that.

As she slept, breathing evenly and so sweetly, I enjoyed the domestic bliss of just being with her. Yes, she was naked, and the sensation of her slim body warm and bare and flush to mine was temptation personified. All I'd need to do would be to nudge her leg a little and slide my dick inside her pussy. Spooning her was torture. Continuing to feel her plump ass against my morning wood was a challenge to resist, but it wasn't only about sex with her. It wasn't only physically that I needed her. I wanted her company because of the simple fact that her presence calmed me. She fit with me, and knowing I had a partner, another half to make me feel complete and whole, was a heady thing to grasp.

This is only the beginning. If I were a smart man about this, I would guarantee every morning would start like this. With her. Peaceful and full of hope.

I had to make her mine. I had to keep her with me. The first step was done. I'd told her that this fake dating stuff was over. It would be real between us, and her future would happen with me.

Time to get busy.

After I slowly extricated myself from her on the bed, moving carefully so as not to disturb her or wake her, I got up and dressed silently. She didn't stir, and I left her cozy in my bed.

I exited my room and headed toward the stairs. Breakfast in bed was due for my woman, but before I went further, I stopped in my tracks in the hallway. Then I doubled back, peering at the doors that would open to her guest room.

She wouldn't be returning here. She belonged in my bed. Considering that I'd need to move her things to my suite, and finally fill the *hers* half of the walk-in closet that had been empty for thirty years, I stepped into her temporary haven.

Nothing lay out, and I was pleased that she was so neat and orderly. A quick peek at her clothes amused me. Eva had no doubt arranged for the purchases of eighty percent of the garments in here, but Nina didn't wear them. I hadn't seen her in any of these designer things. She preferred more laidback clothes, stuff to wear around the house like she would call herself a homebody.

I knew she wasn't materialistic, but this was too funny.

Why bother keeping it all if you have a different preference? I wouldn't ask her. I guessed well enough. She probably didn't want to complain or look ungrateful and just accepted whatever Eva ordered for her.

I snooped. It *wasn't* snooping, since this was my house, she was my woman, and she was getting all these things on my dollar. She wouldn't care if I'd asked to go through her room—that was how confident I was in her closeness with me.

Before I left, I snagged her laptop because it was right there and conveniently within reach.

Downstairs in the kitchen, I placed the laptop on the counter and opened it to boot up. She hadn't set up a lock or password for it. She was that open and not wanting to hold secrets. I took it as a sign of faith and trust in me, and it inspired me to never betray them.

While the browser kicked on and populated what she'd been looking at last, I made coffee. I sat with a mug of the brew and browsed through the tabs she'd left open. Various websites of clothing and other necessities. Even a page for athletic gear suited for running and a fitness watch. In the shopping carts, she'd put many things as "save for later" or on a wish list. Most of the items were only on sale, clearance purchases.

"Fuck that," I mumbled as I chose the brand-new options of all that she'd chosen. Once I moved it all into the cart, I bought it all. While I was at it, I ordered more options, in case she'd struggled to pick things, and then on the one site that offered lingerie, I picked out a variety of sexy apparel I'd love to see her in—for a short while. Until I peeled them off her fine body.

As I sipped my coffee, I woke up with every passing moment. It wasn't only the caffeine erasing the remnants of sleep and making me more alert. It was her. It was the promise of what I could build with her for good. Pampering her was a simple gesture. I had more money than I could ever spend in my lifetime, and using it on her wasn't a challenge. The challenge of finding out ways to please her filled me with energy. I was excited to treat her as well as she could've ever dreamed of experiencing with a lover.

Can it be that simple?

Treat her like a goddess. Knock her up. Marry her. *And keep her.*

It sounded perfect, and I plotted more ways I could show her that I would always provide for her and take care of her. Stefan's warning and the bikers' demands didn't enter my mind. I had too much power for them to win. I had ample security and layers of protection that they'd never get close enough to reach her.

"Morning," Eva said as she entered the kitchen moments later. It seemed like she'd stayed in the main house instead of the guest villa that she called her own home.

"You're up early," I teased. She was not a morning person, at all.

She shrugged, preparing to brew herself a cup of some kind of sugary concoction with caffeine in it. If anyone were to ask me, she put coffee into her creamer, not the other way around.

"Uncle?" She hugged herself and leaned her back against the fridge once she'd set her coffee to brew.

Dammit. I wouldn't begrudge her for wanting my company, but I was annoyed. I'd brought this spare laptop that Nina had been using so I could get a head start on looking into a college she could attend. I'd gotten sidetracked with all the shopping, and I supposed I'd need to wait for another opportunity to research the options close to home.

"Yeah?" I closed the laptop and slid it aside.

"What are you thinking, being with someone like Nina?"

I sighed, hating that she'd ask this again. We'd gone over this. In the first couple of days that Nina had lived here, Eva texted, called, and flat-out confronted me about why this woman was here. I'd told her that we were dating, not wanting to mess with having to explain that we'd been pretending to be a couple. Now, it was a moot point. Nina and I *were* together.

"She's not from our world."

"So?" I leaned back on the stool I'd claimed.

"She's a civilian."

Not for long. The moment I knocked her up or married her, she'd be a Mafia wife through and through.

"She's…"

I held up my hand, deducing from the snarl and disdainful expression on her face that she was ready to unleash more bitter judgment. Eva was orphaned as a young child when my sister and brother-in-law were killed. She was like the daughter I'd never had, but I was well aware of how spoiled and entitled she'd become. A Mafia princess.

"Stop right there," I warned her. "Whatever your bias is with Nina, you need to either get better at swallowing your words or forget about them. I won't stand back and let you question the woman I want in my life. And I won't stand by and listen to you bitching and whining that another woman dares to be here."

"She doesn't fit in."

I stood. "Maybe that's a good thing. Ever look at it that way?"

She had no reply. Instead, she lowered her gaze and twisted her lips into a pout.

"Has she done or said anything to you to warrant your defensiveness or cattiness?"

After a long moment, she shook her head.

"Has she bothered you? Interrupted your plans or life in any way?"

Again, she stalled until shaking her head.

"Is she asking you for help? Begging you to stop what you're doing and—"

"No." She lifted her chin and frowned at me. "No, Uncle. She's not. She's just here, and…"

"She's going to stay, too."

Her brows raised. "How serious is this?" Huffing lightly, she glanced to the side. "I thought… I thought it was some sort of deal. That you'd keep her from Reaper and the bikers as a way to attack them or mess with them."

"No." It felt like a lie. At first, I had offered to date her so the bikers would back off. It wasn't to thwart them, though. It was just because I didn't want her to suffer or be stuck in such a fate.

"You mean it. You actually like her well enough to want to keep her around."

"Yes. Nina is here to stay."

Who I was romantically involved with wasn't any of her business. She wanted to make it her business because she worried about me. Eva was protective of me and Romeo, but she took it too far sometimes. Her default assumption was that everyone was out to get me, to get the Constellas. She was quicker to think someone was conning me than she was to consider the possibility of my being persuaded into matrimony. But there was no room to worry with Nina. She had no ulterior motive—other than to avoid the future her brother almost expected her to suffer.

"Nina isn't going anywhere."

She huffed. "I heard you say that last night."

Exactly.

"She'll be here as long as she wants to be." As I passed her to grab things out of the fridge to start making breakfast, I added, "And you'd damn well better get used to it."

26

NINA

Nina

I stretched in bed, lazy and warm. I hadn't slept that long and that well in so long, even since coming here and living in Dante's house. The bed in the guest room was comfortable, but there was nothing better than sleeping in his arms.

After slapping my hand out and realizing I was alone, I sighed and closed my eyes again.

Was it all a dream? Did I hallucinate after all that champagne and fantasize about his saying he wanted to make it real and keep me in his life for good?

Surprisingly, I wasn't hung over. I sobered up last night, and in the middle of the night, when I woke up and had to go to the restroom, I drank a full glass of water before returning to Dante, where he spooned me and held me close.

I knew we'd talked. I listened to him express his desire to make me his "real" girlfriend, but I was skeptical. It simply sounded too much like a fairytale to believe it. This guardedness couldn't be healthy, but it was the result of how I'd grown up. It was the side effect of facing the trauma and dread of being lost to the MC men.

Before I could sit up and wonder what to do next after sleeping in so long, the door opened.

Dante entered, keeping the wooden panel open by pushing his fine ass against it. And what an ass. Clad in nothing but gray sweatpants, he was a thirst trap, all right. I lost the fight and stared at him, feasting my eyes on his chiseled torso, ripped arms, and cocky smile as he turned toward me.

"Hungry?"

I nodded, thinking of a more carnal sort of starving. I was hungry for him, all right, but it was also sweet of him to bring me breakfast in bed.

"Very hungry."

He used his foot to kick the door shut, and he did it without causing anything on the tray in his hands to wobble. I smelled the coffee, but he'd surpassed that bare minimum of breakfast things. Two plates were covered by silver domes. A bowl of cut fruit slid a bit on the tray, but nothing fell. Nothing spilled.

Except maybe me. I was reminded of my naked status as my arousal began to slip from me. Pushing my thighs together, I did my best not to make a mess on the sheets. But this man just did it for me. The mere sight of him shirtless, those pants slung so low as to give me the visual of the cut lines dipping toward his groin. He turned me on just from breathing and being near.

"Hungry for what?" he challenged.

I still wasn't one hundred percent sure of what his attention meant like this. Was I just a sex toy for him? A convenient woman to keep and fuck when he wanted?

Like that would be so terrible?

All I could do was go with the flow of it and ride this thrill for as long as I could.

A swift streak of naughtiness urged me to show him what I was hungry for. I wanted everything with him, to matter as more than a burden to protect. But right now, seeing him half naked and while I lie in his bed naked...

Bold, but a little nervous, I sat up and flung the covers off me. I slid one foot up the mattress, lifting my knee and giving him a peek of my pussy.

His gaze dropped. He stared and stared, not moving at all as he held the tray in place. "Hungry for what?" he asked again.

The material of his pants pushed up with his dick tenting them, and I parted my legs a little wider. "Hungry for you," I replied, praying I looked sexy and confident, not needy and clueless.

"What are you doing, Nina?" he asked as he set the tray on the table near the bed.

"I was hoping I was seducing you." A little self-deprecating laugh left my lips. "But I'm a novice at it all..."

He growled, staring at my entrance with a smoldering tension. "But if you're hungry," he countered, "that's just a snack for *me*." Crawling onto the bed, he pointed between my legs.

"I meant—"

His deep, throaty chuckle could've been mocking if he was mean like that, but I wasn't sensitive enough to be bothered.

"Tell me what you want," he ordered.

I shrugged, leaning up on my elbows to watch him kneel closer. "Isn't it obvious?"

"Tell me." He glanced up at me as he reached me. Setting his hands on my knees, he smoothed his palms over the joint in a slow caress that also pushed me to widen my legs open.

"You. I want you, Dante."

"Bringing you breakfast in bed?" He lowered, putting his face closer and closer to my pussy.

"It's a sweet thought."

"But in this case," he replied as he moved his head an inch above me, "it's not *that* thought that counts."

"I—"

He was flat on the bed, resting on his stomach. Sliding his hands under my ass, he picked me up and closed another scant inch of distance between my leaking entrance and his smirking mouth. "It's this thought that counts." He pressed his mouth to me, kissing with suction. "Right?"

"Oh, God…" I watched him with a hooded gaze, too stunned and mesmerized with him there to look away.

"I can't read *all* your thoughts, Nina. Tell me what you want."

I'd never been forward like this. Not sexually. I lost my virginity to him, and my experience revolved around him. Only him.

He wanted me to just say it? Out loud? Why couldn't he read me so well that he wouldn't have to ask? I wasn't sure I could be *this* forward and direct.

"Tell me," he taunted, gazing up at me.

"I want…" I bit my lower lip, intimidated.

"Every time you do that…" he growled. He pressed his mouth to my pussy and nipped near my clit, along my folds.

"Oh, my God!" I damn near vaulted off the bed.

"Sexy, Nina. Every time you tease your lip like that and bite it, it makes me want to do the same." Again, he put his mouth on me and sucked the flesh near my clit, then he swiped his tongue up and down, soothing away the sting.

"More, Dante. I want your mouth on me. Right there."

"Say it, Nina." He teased me, licking and flicking the tip of his tongue at my clit. "Tell me."

"Suck me. Lick my pussy." A rush of heat spread over my cheeks. It wasn't humiliating, but instead, freeing. Admitting what I wanted was a new adventure of going for it too.

He didn't delay. His fingers bit into my ass as he hoisted me up, and smashing his face to me, he drove me all the way to a swift, intense orgasm. He licked from my entrance to my clit. His mouth suctioned and kissed, but when he sucked on my clit, I was done for.

"Dante. Fuck. Dante!" Gibberish came next, and as I panted and gasped through the waves of extreme pleasure of my release, I didn't know—and didn't care—what the hell I was saying anymore.

He didn't stay down there. Crawling up, he shifted to the side to remove his pants. Commando. He didn't have to give up any more time to remove his boxers. Naked and hard, he shifted me onto my hands and knees.

"Tell me what you want, Nina."

It was an order, not a suggestion. While I still came down from the high of coming once, I was still aroused. I was still eager to share my body with him, to give myself up to him.

"I want…" I licked my lips as I rose onto my knees. It was a shaky lift, but his arms snaked around me and held me steady. I reveled in the friction of his hard chest against my back, but I refused to get too limp and lazy, sated and satisfied.

"Tell me," he ordered.

An incredulous yet weak laugh escaped me. "Why? You'd give me anything I asked for?"

He gripped my chin and turned me to face him. The kiss he gave me rendered me breathless and needy. "Yes," he replied. Simple and to the point, and I wanted to believe him.

"I want this," I said as I lowered my hand and slipped it between our thighs. Gripping his hard dick, I wrapped my fingers around his hard length and stroked the soft erection.

"Take it." He groaned as I squeezed slightly tighter and pumped him a little faster.

Do you really mean that? To be my lover, not just my provider? To be my man, my boyfriend, and not just the powerful leader who can save me from those bikers?

"I want it deep inside me."

He growled, kissing me roughly and quickly as he dipped his body lower. The fat cockhead pushed at my sensitive entrance, still throbbing from the magic of his masterful mouth there. Then with a lift and a cinching hug of his arms holding me against his front, he stabbed up and slid all the way into me.

Seated to the hilt, he speared up inside my pussy. I groaned at the stretch, breathing through the shock of how full it felt. A good fullness, one that urged me to beg for him to move and caress me so intimately.

"Are you going to take it?" he asked.

"Give it to me, Dante." I was getting onboard with this filthy talk. "Fuck me now."

He chuckled, loosening his arms from my waist and chest to urge me to lower. Back on my hands again, the angle of his dick driving into me felt deeper and different. Then lower yet, my breasts swayed with his pounding force as I leaned down onto my forearms. Realizing my nipples could get attention by rubbing over the sheet, I inched lower yet.

"Take it all, Nina."

I nodded, smushing my face against the bed as he pushed on my shoulders until my ass was up in the air. Stretched with my arms out, I was tilted all the way down. He didn't stop once, ramming into me with such speed and power that his balls smacked my ass and his thighs braced against mine with each push in.

His hands stayed on my hips. Crescents would show from his nails digging into my skin there, but I didn't mind the pain. They served as pinpricks of awareness while he bulldozed over all my senses. With his hard cock slamming into my cunt, sucked in with my juices and squeezing him tight, I couldn't think. I felt him everywhere, and as I came again, he smacked my ass and roared.

"Yes, Nina. Like that. Fuck. Milk my goddamn cock."

I closed my eyes, aware that my drool would stick to the mattress. That was how messy we were. He'd reduced me to a pool of bliss, overtaken by ecstasy and the utter relief of all my nerve endings exploding with the wave of this orgasm. I grunted something, or maybe it was another groaned-out word. I didn't know.

In the next moment, he came, squeezing my flesh to hold on. His dick jerked inside me, filling me with his hot cum. Back and forth, he rocked some more, but slower and without the fierce urgency that he'd used to get us here.

Leaning forward, he slumped on me. His chest heaved against my back. Droplets of sweat fell to my hair. Hunched over together, we dragged in ragged breaths and tried to calm our hearts from the rush.

"Is that what you wanted?" he asked moments later as he slid out of me.

I couldn't help the faint moan as he slipped out. I was so sensitive yet. "Yeah, it was." I kneeled up to face him with him standing next to the bed.

Like ridiculous fools, we grinned at each other. Sated, satisfied, and best of all, comfortable together.

I could only hope it would last, like he claimed it should.

27

DANTE

Dante

For the next two weeks, Nina and I built on the real connection between us. No more pretending anything. No excuses of practicing for anything else.

Before, the deal was that we had to put on an act in front of others. Now, our deal was that we didn't want to leave each other's company long enough to bother with anyone else.

She moved into my room, pleased and flattered that I'd gone ahead and bought her the things she actually wanted. Not the wardrobe and appearance that Eva assumed she should have to fit in with me.

I kept her at my side in bed every night, and each morning, I spent several minutes watching her sleep in and be lazy, naked and sated, the same as I was.

Franco joked that we had claimed an unofficial honeymoon, and Romeo smirked in such a knowing way that suggested he agreed.

I made myself scarce, handling calls with Nina in the room with me. While I kept up with my meetings, having Franco and Romeo filling me in on the essentials of the organization, I had those meetings only at the house and when Nina was near.

We worked out together. Cooked together. Slept together.

Best of all, though, was how she came alive and really thrived under my tutelage. I'd never forget the "lessons" where I taught her how I wanted her to give me head. I bet neither of us would lose the memory of when we incorporated some toys and vibrators to further and double her orgasms. Mine too.

After decades of settling for random flings here and there, one-night stands that I forgot about as soon as they were over, Nina gave me a chance to revisit the concept of love.

"Do you think you can pay attention?" Franco joked.

We sat outside at our favorite patio table. With the summer heat unrelenting, Nina opted to swim laps in the pool while we talked. Seeing her in my peripheral vision was a hex. In that skimpy bikini, the tanned swells of her breasts glistening from the water, all that long, brown hair in sexy, tousled waves...

I cleared my throat, annoyed that they'd caught me staring. "Yeah. Of course. What were you saying?"

Romeo laughed and scooted his chair to the side, further blocking Nina from my line of sight.

Just as well. My focus isn't worth a damn when she's swimming so close.

"The Devil's Brothers' men have made a habit of coming into the Hound and Tea rooms more often." Franco lost his teasing smirk, scowling as he repeated this news. "The security staff are turning them away, but sometimes, they come without their usual biker clothes and sneak in disguised as others."

I shook my head, more than peeved about this. "I never wanted them in there in the first place."

"They never should have come into those rooms." Romeo zoned out, stuck staring at his water glass covered in beads of condensation on the table. "It's only with invitation that anyone gets in the doors to begin with."

"Yeah, but when the Dominos tried to stand up to the bikers with those drug deals, it seemed they turned our gambling rooms into common grounds, a neutral zone to meet or argue."

That was the only way the MC men got their feet in the door. Someone from the Domino organization likely told Reaper or his other bikers to meet at the Hound and Tea. None of the Mafia members would've willingly met up or discussed anything at the motorcycle gang's clubhouse, and none of the bikers would've volunteered to set foot on the Domino turf.

"Unless Stefan facilitated the MC men coming to the gambling rooms," I said. "He allied with the Dominos, so maybe it was his role to set up meets. And he chose the Hound and Tea rooms to host them."

Franco nodded. "That wouldn't surprise me."

"It does add up," Romeo said. He yawned and rubbed the back of his neck. "He brought them into the Sarround Gala. He could've coaxed them to become regulars at the gambling rooms too."

"Regardless of how or why those fuckers got in, they've overstayed their stay. It's time for them to understand the doors will remain closed to them—for good."

"So far, it hasn't caused issues," Franco said.

I shot him a rotten look. "No issues?"

Romeo scoffed. "You forget about Ricky Bardot betting on Nina there? With Reaper?"

Franco winced. "Well, that."

That was a very critical issue for me, personally. "By the way, has anyone seen him recently?"

"Reaper?" Franco guessed at the same time Romeo asked, "Ricky?"

I pointed at my son. "Ricky."

Both of them shook their heads.

"I've asked around," Franco replied. "Ever since Nina came to live here with you, she became a case, and I've had men looking for intel about Ricky."

"Same," Romeo reported. "When Nina mentioned that he'd bet on her with Reaper—"

"She told you?" I asked.

He rolled his eyes. "When I drove her home from Escott's. She blurted out how she'd come across you."

He's known that long. That we started out as faking it all.

Yet, the knowing smirk he gave me suggested that he hadn't bought it.

"I've had people looking for him," Romeo added. "In case he tried to reach Nina and still hand her over to Reaper."

"Has she heard from him?" Franco asked.

"Once," I answered. "She showed me the text he sent her, but other than that, no calls, no texts, no voicemails."

Romeo shrugged. "Makes me wonder if maybe the MC took him. If they could try to use Ricky as a hostage to get Nina to come to them."

I narrowed my eyes and shook my head. "I doubt it. We've started to talk a bit more about her past. She loves her brother in the name of caring about her sibling, but they've never been close."

"They shared an apartment," Franco said.

"Yes, because he mooched off me for money," Nina said, clearly unwilling to let us talk about her. She approached, coming into view around Romeo. A thick towel was tied snug around her waist. With another, smaller towel, she dried the moisture from her hair. "Sorry. I heard my name and listened."

I scooted my chair back for her to sit on my lap. She was my woman, always would be, so it wasn't difficult to let her in on this conversation. She was loyal to a fault, but to me.

"If the MC takes Ricky and tries to negotiate, to get me to go to Reaper in exchange for freeing Ricky…" She licked her lips and lifted her finger. "One, I'm not that stupid. They wouldn't release him."

Exactly.

"Two, it's karma. Ricky tried to hand me over to them, and it would only be justice for him to go to them instead."

It sounded cold, but firm. That was the strong woman who had my heart.

"And three," she said, lifting the third finger, "they'd have to get past *him* to reach me." She patted my cheek, smug.

I caught her hand and kissed her palm. "Well said."

"However, we shouldn't be this lax about the Devil's Brothers coming to the Hound and Tea," Romeo said.

I suspected he said that with a figment of that stubborn survivor's guilt he still struggled with. That if he could help spare men from a worse fate, he would join in on the action immediately.

"Then I'll go have a word with them," I replied matter-of-factly.

Nina stood from my lap. "Tonight?"

I nodded. "The sooner, the better."

She kissed me quickly. "Then hopefully, I'll be back when you are."

"That's right. Your spa day."

She smiled wide. "I think it might be fun. I've never had a 'spa' day before. It was nice of Eva to ask me along."

Romeo rolled his eyes. "She probably just wants to justify going herself."

Nina shrugged. "Well, I appreciate the invite. I'm looking forward to it."

I was too. If she came home relaxed, it would be the perfect motivation to get her all excited again, on my cock.

Later, Romeo accompanied me on the way to the Hound and Tea. I hadn't been back here since that night Nina literally ran into me here. I had no reason. Actually, now that we had jumped into our relationship, I seldom made time for many visits. Romeo seemed to benefit from handling the things I used to. I wasn't anywhere near ready to hand over the reins of the organization to him, but as he coped with the night those three soldiers were killed, being busy and not having time to dwell were a positive outcome.

He spoke with the security staff as we reached the back doors. Two men were perturbed, pissed that word had come back to them of two bikers sneaking inside.

"I'll handle it," I told them. And I would. I didn't expect lower-level bouncers and security guards at the door to tell the leader of another crime unit to back off and not come back. That was a task best delegated to me. One leader managing another. Man to man.

It helped that Reaper was there. If it was a couple of his men, my message wouldn't have been as direct. It was preferred to tell that MC fucker to the face to get the hell out of my gambling rooms, and to stay away.

He wasn't easily recognizable dressed in more basic clothes. Without the grungy, dusty leather vest and all the colorful patches sewn on it, he almost blended in. Instead of ripped and filthy jeans, he chose slacks to complement the cheap suit he'd picked up somewhere. The signature bandana wasn't tied on his head, and the slicked-back effect of the little thinning hair he had might have been presentable on someone else.

His eyes didn't lie. As he met my gaze from across the room, he sneered with pure malice. This asshole would always be up to no good. Kicking him out would be my pleasure.

"Get out." That was my greeting. It was the only order I had in mind, too. In one fell swoop, I conveyed all that needed to be said.

"Fuck off," he replied cockily. "What's a man gotta do to get a fucking drink around here?" He tapped his fist to the top of the bar he was leaning against.

When the bartender glanced at me, I shook my head. The smart man backed up.

"Get out of my gambling rooms. Get out of my life, you ugly piece of shit."

Reaper stood straighter, cocking his head side to the side and cracking the kinks. "How about... no?"

I grabbed the front of his pathetic shirt. "Reconsider your answer." Lifting him slightly, I made sure to tower over him and let him notice that I had significant weight and bulk on him—all in muscles.

"I'm not reconsidering shit. I got a right to be here."

"No, you don't." Romeo straightened his cuffs. "We decide who is allowed up here."

"Oh, just like you think you fancy Mafia sons of bitches can decide that you can take my girl."

"She's not your girl," I growled through clenched teeth.

"I won her—"

I tightened my fingers, fisting more of his too-loose shirt that didn't fit him. Bunching up more of the fabric had me damn near strangling him with a binding over his neck.

"Give her up, Constella." He snarled at me, spittle flying. "I won her fair and square."

Without releasing him, I waited for a moment to reply. I wanted him to think that I was searching for something to say, something to argue, but I already knew my ace card in this deal.

Slanting closer, to keep this between us alone, I almost gave in to a smile. "Are you sure you want a woman pregnant with *my* kid?"

He bared his teeth, wrenching out of my grip. I let him go and shook off my fingers, as though to rid the taint of touching him.

"The fuck?" he demanded. "You knocked her up?"

Now I let my grin show. He would do well to take notice of how triumphant I felt about that topic. "If she's not knocked up yet, she will be before I'm done with her."

Nina meant far more to me than being the potential mother of my child. I already had Romeo. I had someone to share my legacy with, someone to pass it on to. If Nina were to have my baby, I would be happy. Over the moon. Excited.

It wasn't a prerequisite to keeping her with me. Sure, the presence of a baby would strengthen her connection to me. It would make it that much harder for anyone to try to take her from me.

I wanted her for her. Because she was the sweet, easygoing, and generous woman that she was.

At the rate we were going, she'd be so full of my cum from getting it daily that she was simply bound to be pregnant sooner or later. And since she was well aware that we weren't using protection, she was fine with taking that risk.

I snapped my fingers, not taking my focus off Reaper as he fumed. Constella soldiers surrounded him and his friend, and with minimal struggle, they had them restrained to toss out.

"Don't come back. This had better be the last I'll ever see of you," I warned.

He spat at me. The disgusting glob landed on the carpet, just missing my shoes. "I wouldn't count on it."

That sounded like a threat, but I didn't scare easily. This MC was past due to leave the area, and I was glad to be able to contribute to exiling them, at least from my businesses.

Good riddance, motherfucker.

I wanted the Devil's Brothers to be a thing of the past so I could be free to concentrate on my future with Nina.

28

NINA

Nina

Eva and I arrived at the spa without any issues.

An hour into it, relaxing after a thorough massage, I sank against the cushions of a couch in the spa's lounging area and sighed.

"I feel like a puddle."

Eva nodded, stretching back as she moaned lightly. "It's been a while since I've felt this loose."

"It's... world changing," I joked. "I never realized a massage could be *this* good." Good, but still not as good as sex with Dante. Or his brand of massage that he liked to give me. Any time that sexy man had his hands on me was a gift.

She glanced at me as the spa staff member brought us our iced waters. "You've never had one?"

I shook my head, then sipped. Even the water tasted better somehow.

The masseuse liquified me with that deep tissue kneading, and I was parched.

"Never had the money."

Eva raised her brows. "You do now, cozying up with my uncle."

I didn't flinch. I was sick of her mean girl routine, but I'd started to think she was lightening up on me.

Guess not.

"I'm not a gold-digger, Eva." I sipped more water. "I'm not the bad guy no matter how desperate you are to see me as the villain."

She didn't double down with the attack. Instead, she nodded. "I just want to make sure."

I shrugged. If I hadn't convinced her to not be a bitch to me by now, there was nothing else I could do to salvage the situation. "If you loathe me so much, why'd you invite me along tonight?"

"I don't loathe you. And I can tell you're not a gold-digger. I went through your guest room." She smirked. "You haven't even touched any of the clothes I ordered for you."

I laughed lightly, too relaxed to find the energy to show my amusement completely. "No, I didn't. I had to wear those dresses when Dante told me to. But he ordered me things more my preference—"

"Cheaper, you mean."

I shrugged one shoulder. "We have different tastes. That's not a crime."

"I suppose."

"Why do you keep giving me a hard time if you know I'm not a materialist user trying to take advantage of Dante?"

"Because he's suffered through women like that before, one-night stands who got it in their heads that he'd be their sugar daddy."

Her saying that reminded me of that time Tessa and I joked about it. Sugar daddies. Dante wasn't one. He was... my boyfriend.

Speak of the devil. My phone chimed with another text, and I frowned as I pulled it out of my purse while Eva chattered.

"Many women have looked at my uncle—and my cousin—as easy ways to get rich."

"He has yet to give me any money," I told her.

"But all his flings—"

Before I looked at my phone, I shot her a look.

"What, you don't like me mentioning that he's slept around?" she taunted.

"He's had sex before. I'm well aware. He's much older than me, but I think you're overexaggerating. Dante was married to his job, to the family's businesses and deals, before I moved in."

She huffed. "You're right about that."

"His not being quite the player you're making him out to be?"

"That. But also that he's changed his workaholic habits since you showed up."

I couldn't keep up the lies anymore. Weeks ago, after that ill-fated evening at Escott's, I blurted out to Romeo that Dante and I were pretending to be a couple. I never told Eva. Even though Dante and I weren't faking anything anymore, I felt bad not to explain to his niece.

"When Dante and I met, we agreed to a fake date. We were pretending to be together so I wouldn't have to go to the Devil's Brothers."

She scrunched her face. "Why would you?"

"My brother bet using me and lost me to Reaper."

She rolled her eyes. "What an idiot."

"An idiot I cut ties with when I ran into Dante that night."

"You haven't talked to your brother since he lost his bet to the biker leader?"

I shook my head. "No."

She grimaced.

"I'm sorry to have kept that from you. And I know you'll assume I *am* conning someone by explaining why I moved into the house at all."

"Oh, please." She waved me off and laughed once. "It might have started out like that, a fake relationship, but it's pretty damn clear that my uncle wants you for real."

I smiled. It sure looked like that. It felt like it too. A smidgen of doubt lingered, though, and I hated that I would always be this guarded in life.

My phone buzzed again, and I cringed as I looked at it, pulled from this conversation with Eva.

"Who's been calling you all night?" she asked.

"It's not calls. Just old voicemails that are blank and texts that won't load. It's an old phone."

"My uncle will get you a new one," she said.

I was sure he would, but I didn't want to ask. This one worked—or it did until it seemed to want to die today.

"Well, who is it?"

"My friend. Tessa. We used to waitress at the steakhouse together." I bit my lip and tried to call her again. It dropped.

"Is something wrong?"

"I worry that something is. She's been pressured to marry this creep. He's a lawyer, and her parents are pushing her to get hitched because they think that means *they'd* get money. I'm nervous that he's going to force her to elope or something."

Eva shook her head. "That's bullshit."

"And now that we mentioned my brother, I realize he wouldn't be able to contact me if this phone is toast. I don't remember his number." My peaceful sluggishness faded. Anxiety crept back in. "He's an asshole, and I say karma should be served for his losing me in a bet. For betting with my life in the first place!"

"I'd say," Eva said.

"But he *is* my brother. The only family I have left. When my dad was dying in the hospice, he made me promise to look after Ricky."

"Wait, is he an older or younger brother?"

"Older." I tucked my hair behind my ear. "But that doesn't matter. He's still family. I tried, but…"

Eva shocked me, reaching out to pat my knee. "Hey, it'll work out however it's supposed to."

"Wow. Did they slip a sedative into your water? Are you actively trying to be *nice* to me?"

She smirked. "Yeah. I can't help it. I'm glad that you care about others. I see it in the way you interact with my uncle. Hearing you worry about your friend, and even your brother, who doesn't deserve kindness for losing you in a bet to the MC…" She smiled, almost sheepish to do so. "I like that you're not self-centered."

"Thanks. That means a lot."

She must have met her quota for sappy topics and sharing her feelings. Furrowing her brow, she concentrated. "Is your friend stuck in an arranged marriage?"

"No. Not formally. Just caught between persuasive people who just want to use her, I think."

"Some families *only* pair up with arranged marriages."

"That sounds like hell."

She nodded, flicking her perfectly smooth hair back over her shoulder. "Oh, it is."

"You haven't been arranged with anyone?"

Her responding bark of laughter was haughty. "No. My uncle would *never* make that choice for me."

"But it does happen?" I wasn't thinking about Dante or myself. Not even Eva or Romeo. For some reason, I was looking ahead. *If I were to have a child with him...would my baby be expected to marry someone chosen for them?*

I wasn't sure if I was getting *too* far ahead of myself. With every day that my period was late, I grew more excited with the prospect that I could already be pregnant. If I wasn't, I had to be infertile. Dante and I were having sex at least once, but usually multiple times, daily. We'd never used protection, and it felt like it was bound to happen sooner or later.

If I was late any longer, I'd ask for a test. When I worked my ass off, always waitressing, I seldom got my cycles. The stress. The constant working. Poor sleep. I never worried because I was a virgin. Now that I wasn't, the absence of my period could mean something. Something permanent.

"Nina." Eva cleared her throat, breaking the silence of several minutes by saying my name.

"Yeah?" I stuck my phone in my pocket, giving up on it for now. I'd have to ask Dante for one tonight. I didn't want to be without a means of calling him.

"You do realize that Ricky's not contacting you might mean..." She winced, raising her brows in a prompt for me to finish her statement.

I sighed. "Yes. I considered that. I don't want to think about it. If the MC was mad that he didn't hand me over, they could've done anything to him." Horrible, unfathomable things like torture.

Or murder.

"Maybe Dante can look into it for you," she offered.

I almost smiled. "He did tell me that I could ask him for anything."

She snorted a laugh. "Yeah, he's infatuated with you. He'd give you the world if he could."

Warmth filled me, and deep inside, I felt at peace. He really did care for me. I knew it from the bottom of my heart.

"You're prepared to commit to him?" she asked. "For the long haul?"

Considering the way I'm wondering if I have his baby inside me already, yes, in for the long haul. I nodded.

"What do you want with him?" she asked, but not sounding pushy about it.

"I want it all," I answered.

"Do you love him?"

Very much. I nodded. As I opened my mouth, ready to admit it, I was startled. Franco ran up to us, dashing through the spa. Blood spilled down his shirt.

"Franco?" He was shot!

Another Constella guard sprinted with him, but a gunshot rang out and the man fell forward.

Eva screamed. The staff at the spa yelled and shrieked as well, scattering and running or ducking to hide from the men running in, the gunfire, and the guard dropping to the floor to lie unmoving.

"Go!" Franco ordered me.

More shots were fired, and as Eva moved to stand, to run, reaching out for my hand to guide me to safety with her, I flinched as a bullet sank into the cushion of the couch. Inches from my head. It was the luckiest miss, but I wasn't sure Eva would survive a hit if she got up from the shelter of this lounge area.

"Get down!" I yelled it as I pushed Eva down, sparing her from a direct hit to the head, given the location of where the bullet pierced through the chair she'd sat in.

As we stumbled lower from my act of shoving her and covering for her, I lost my balance.

I fell. It was such a hard impact that my breath was punched out of me. I'd been holding it, tense and bracing for pain with this sudden attack.

My head smacked on the edge of the low table, and darkness quickly eased into my vision, sending me to oblivion as I was knocked unconscious.

29

DANTE

Dante

I stayed at the Hound and Tea long enough to see that Reaper and his gnarly friend were tossed out. The security staff consisted of professionals, and it wasn't anything as dramatic as dragging the bikers out by the collars of their ugly shirts.

They kept their hands on them as they ushered them to the door, and from the third floor windows, I watched the pair of MC members get in a car and speed off.

"I would've thought they'd come on their bikes," Romeo said. He stood next to me, watching the pair leave.

"I bet they have all manner of vehicles for disguises." Just like how they snuck in here, dressing up more like the usual clientele that gambled here. I turned away, satisfied that they'd left. I had no doubt they'd try to come back. The Devil's Brothers would be a problem until they were all six feet under.

"I want more men on it. Follow all their vehicles. Track them."

Romeo nodded, leaving with me.

"I want to know how many of these fuckers are in that club." *Because if I've got to be the one to rid the world of them, I'll need to prepare accordingly.*

"Everything. I want to know every single fucking thing about them. You and Franco have already started to gather intel about them. Now is the time to step it up."

"On it."

Romeo drove off in a different direction, likely one of the other properties he preferred when he didn't want to stay at the mansion. That was where I headed, impatient to see Nina. She was the reward I could look forward to after dealing with scum like Reaper.

On the drive, I thought back to how I'd referred to her—potentially knocked up. That was another way of belittling her. She wasn't here just to bear my child. She wasn't important in my life just because thrusting into her pussy was a lot like coming home.

She was a friend. A support system. A listening and level-headed woman who would make a good partner, even outside the bedroom.

Is that why she's still so guarded? Over the last couple of weeks, we'd fucked almost nonstop. It was, like Franco had teased, a honeymoon period where we couldn't get enough of each other. While connecting in a physical way was easy and enjoyable, I realized that she still maintained a slight edge of distance, as though she was waiting for the other shoe to drop.

It wouldn't. But how would she know? I told her I wanted to keep her with me forever. I was clear that we weren't pretending anything anymore.

I had yet to express how I *felt*, though, the more emotionally charged kind of relationship.

Love. I hadn't given her an indication that all I did for her and wanted to give her was an act of love.

"Time to fix that mistake," I muttered as I pulled into the drive. I didn't want Nina to go another moment of thinking she was just someone to fuck consistently.

Inside, I didn't see any sign of her. But the person who was waiting for me in my bedroom pissed me off.

"What the fuck are you doing here?" I narrowed my eyes at Vanessa sitting on a chair near my and Nina's closets. That piece of furniture would be removed and destroyed, now tainted from her being in this place and touching the cushion.

She had no right to be in here, no allowance to be present on the property at all, much less inside the home I now shared with Nina.

"Welcome home, Dante." She smiled slowly. It was a practiced expression meant to make men drool and drop to their knees. Seductive and cunning, that was how I could sum it up. She'd given me this very same smile countless other times, and it always resulted in the same reaction—anger and annoyance.

"Cut the sex-kitten bullshit. What the fuck are you doing in here?"

She stood, uncurling from her perch on the chair. Her hair was down but curled expertly. The long coat she covered her body with prevented her from emphasizing the sway of her hips or the curves of the body she'd gone under the scalpel for.

When she shrugged it off her shoulders, revealing her nudity, I saw it all.

She was throwing herself at me. Breaking in, trespassing in this room that Nina belonged in, and offering herself without any modesty.

"I'm here to show you what you're missing," she purred as she approached me.

"I'm not missing anything. How did you get in here?" I refused to lower my gaze and notice her naked body. Keeping my stare locked on hers, I waited for her to see the severity of how she was fucking up with this stunt. I was livid, and only a slight purse of her lips suggested that she understood that.

"Who let you in?" All the staff knew not to permit her past the gates.

"I let myself in." She slowed at a table and picked up a key. "Daddy had a copy made for me."

Mother fucking Stefan. He went too damn far. "Get out of here." I'd *just* told Reaper that at the gambling rooms. It seemed tonight was all about exorcizing the idiots I didn't have patience for.

"Dante, you don't know what you're saying."

"I do." I shoved my hands in my pants' pockets, too familiar with her tendency to reach out and grab my hands to pull herself closer to me. It was a trick she did all the time in public settings. I would do anything I could to remove her ammunition or access to slinking up too close for comfort.

"Please, Dante." She did it now, stretching her hand out to wrap her fingers around my elbow.

I turned, shoving out of her reach. "No. You're not going to gaslight me. You're not going to seduce me or manipulate me. You never have. I told you every fucking time you approached that I wasn't interested, and you're overdue to understand that when I say no, it means fucking no."

"Please!" She dropped to her knees and reached for my zipper.

Jumping back, I twisted my hips so she couldn't make another grab for me like that.

She scrambled back to her feet, lunging at me. "You need me," she pleaded. Her arms winched around me, and I quickly shoved her back.

Nothing worked. She did nothing for me, and this desperation that she showed seemed too bizarre. Too unhinged.

I held her at arm's length, not trusting her not to come on to me and grab me again. Although I hated to have any physical contact with her at all, I had to keep her where she could look at me and listen.

And explain. Red flags were flying with her behavior, and I started to assume the worst.

If she was here, the one time Nina wasn't… *What else did she plan?* It was no coincidence, her letting herself in when Nina wasn't present.

"You've always wanted me, Dante. You know you have."

I shook my head. "I want Nina."

She grimaced, annoyed. "She's gone."

Fuck! I gritted my teeth and adjusted my stance with her. Instead of gripping her upper arms, the rage burning inside me fueled me to slide my fingers around her neck. Hoisting her up, choking her, I waited until she set her panicked gaze on me to see that I wasn't playing around. Her legs kicked and flailed, and she clawed at my fingers over her throat.

"What did you do?"

She tried to shake her head. Tears glossed over her eyes, and as she struggled to breathe, deprived of the ability to inhale, she smacked at my hand.

"Tell me!" I released her with a fling. She flew back, down to the floor, and wheezed for air as she sat there.

"Tell me *now*."

She crawled toward her coat, coughing and catching her breath. "Stefan needs your help."

"He's not getting a single fucking thing from me. I've made myself clear."

She swallowed hard as she pulled her coat on, avoiding me. "He lost too much money from allying with the Domino Family. When they were finished, broken up or killed, he lost all the investments. He's had to give up many of his assets to stay afloat."

I shook my head, wondering why she was giving me this sob story.

"If you marry me, he can have some of your money."

"There isn't a chance in hell of that ever happening."

"And if I don't get you to marry me..." She sniffled as she stood. "He'll give me to the MC. He'll hand me over to the Devil's Brothers. They put a price on me, but Stefan seems to think they're lowballing."

This woman was forced to discuss her *price*. To own up to a future of being sold. I shook my head, frustrated and furious that Stefan would stoop this low. With his own daughter. With his former friend. I hadn't needed any other reasons to cast him out of my life, but he was giving me more and more motivation to hate him every day.

A soldier rushed to the open doors. He stopped short, volleying his gaze between me and Vanessa. "The gates reported—"

I pointed at her. "Get her out of here." I shoved past him, having heard enough.

I had to get Nina.

If Vanessa had timed her break-in and seductive act for tonight, it meant she'd counted on Nina being gone and staying out of the house long enough for her to try.

I ran downstairs, ready to drive to the spa Eva had chosen for a girls' night. With every step, fear and anger mixed into a heady swarm of violent emotions. And I let it shroud me. I let the rage seep through my bones and give me the drive to capture and kill.

If anything happened to the woman I wanted to spend the rest of my life with, no one would be able to stop me from burning down the world in retaliation.

30

NINA

Nina

I woke up quickly. It was a dizzying, blurring distortion of all my senses, and I panicked when I couldn't immediately tell where I was, what was happening, and who was to blame for this attack.

My vision was cloudy and limited. My tongue felt heavy in my dry mouth, and as I rolled to my side, my stomach roiled and threatened to send bile up my throat. Worst was how my head pounded at the tender ache on the back of my skull. Lifting my hand to touch the massive lump forming under my hair, I realized how shaky and uncoordinated I was in moving my arm.

This was no instant rebound. I was sluggish and so confused. But I knew enough that I would be all right. Once I figured out where the hell I was, I'd get out of this scrape. I knew it. Or I wanted to believe that sort of optimism and confidence.

I had to get out of this dark warehouse I'd been transferred to. I *had* to. Because I had to get back to Dante. We'd only just begun our lives together, and it was far too soon to lose him. To lose what we could be.

The determination to get back to Dante was all the motivation I needed to shove back the nausea and discomfort from falling.

Without sitting up, I opened my eyes and looked around at this old, dirty place. Old beer signs lay broken and busted in a heap in the corner. A mountain of empty liquor bottles sat at the other end of the wall opposite me. In the distance, I heard the telltale music and chatter combination that signaled I was at a bar.

Maybe?

Despite just being knocked out, I could easily piece together what happened.

I'd heard those men on the second floor at the gala, talking about kidnapping me so Vanessa could have Dante. I witnessed Stefan arguing with Dante that I had to go back to Reaper and be handed over to the MC. With those clues, I figured that this had to be their building, maybe their clubhouse, where they met and partied. It would explain the rowdy sounds of a bar nearby.

He'll find me. I clung to that fact as I heard men walking and talking in this dark, dirty room. It wasn't a warehouse, but more like a storage space. And in the darkness, I did all that I could to bring me back to Dante, to facilitate my coming home to him.

He would notice when I didn't come home. Franco would alert him too. There was no way this could turn into a missing persons case. Dante was too possessive of me to have to sleuth out how to locate me.

Grabbing my derelict phone, I tried to help. I couldn't be sure it worked. It was mostly malfunctioning, but I prayed that pressing and holding the button on the side would open the camera app. And once in there, that one swipe of my thumb to the left would choose the video option. Groping in the dark, not wanting to move too much to give away that I was awake and recording them, I pressed my finger at where I hoped the *record* button would be on the screen.

"I don't know, man," one said. "Reaper's fucking nuts if he thinks we can go after the motherfucking Constellas."

Another man laughed, dark and sinister, before he coughed. "What, like it can't be done?"

"I don't think they'd go down as easily as the Domino outfit did."

"The Dominos were weak," a third man said, laughing.

"Pussies hardly fought back at all, even with Giovanni supposedly fighting alongside them," the second man replied.

"Yeah, and now, Stefan's trying to switch sides and two-time *us*," the first man added.

"You think Reaper will string him along for too long?" someone else asked. "We got this Nina bitch, now, and that's gonna be the trigger to make Dante come at us—"

"Nah, nah, nah," the second man said. "We ain't gonna keep her. We'll give her back once he pays up. Give her back in pieces."

They all laughed and carried on, talking about how they'd use me as a pawn in their war. The Giovanni Family wasn't trusted by anyone, not by Dante, and not by this motorcycle gang as they tried to convince him they were friends now. So much of what they boasted about made no sense. I hoped, again, that I was recording it because it seemed like these bikers were talking freely and honestly.

Come on, Dante. Please. Look for my phone. Storm down the gates of their club. He couldn't be far, but I worried my time was running out. Stalling was all good and well, but the men in this storage room got impatient.

"You're not too bad on the eyes," one biker said as he crept closer, eyeing me like he wanted to rape me.

"Even if she was..." Another man walked up and tossed a burlap sack to his buddy. "She ain't gotta look at us."

"Fuck off," I snapped, scrambling back toward the wall.

Please, Dante. Please, please, please *hurry.* If these assholes got it in their mind to rape me, to share me...

Bile shot up my throat again. The threat of a gang rape was too horrid, too unspeakable, and my body revolted.

"I want to see her as I fuck her."

"Not before I do."

"You get her ass. I'll take her pussy."

"Fuck that. She's going to gag on my cock first."

They bickered, all coming closer to surround me. Cornered like this, I had no chance to run. Outnumbered like this, I had no option to fight back.

Please, please, please. I wanted to save myself, but I was without a single resource or weapon.

"He'll kill you," I said, hoping that psychological warfare would make an impact.

It didn't. They all cracked up, laughing and taunting me more with my threat. Dante would, though, and I had enough faith to know that he *had* to be on his way to me. All the Constella men would rally with their leader.

Fate couldn't be so cruel. I couldn't have found him only to lose him this soon.

"You're going to be a good little bitch and—"

The biker never finished his statement. As I cowered and shrank back from him standing over me, his head burst apart. Blood and gray matter splattered, forced toward the wall.

I turned my head and screamed, not wanting anything to rain into my open mouth. Gunfire filled the room, and I tucked into the tightest ball that I could. Smoke and screams came. Men shouted and yelled. Threats were shouted. The music stopped, and without risking to open my eyes and witness the utter violence taking over, I knew that my wishes had come true.

In dark, morbid detail, my rescue had happened. Or it would. I recognized the yells from the Constella men I was already becoming more familiar with. The guards and soldiers who swore loyalty to Dante. I felt the vibrations sending up from the wooden floor I lay on, wishing a hole could open up and swallow me down so I wouldn't get hit by a body or a bullet.

Footsteps pounded every which way as the place was stormed and became crowded. Thuds reverberated from the walls as bodies were slammed and shoved. Wet streaks splattered constantly, and I sucked in a sob, keeping my mouth shut as I knew those were more globs of blood and other bodily fluids. Screaming with my lips clamped tight, I shook and tensed, balling up into the smallest form against the wall that I could.

Trying to block out all my senses, I fell into a numb status. I retreated into the darkness behind my squinted-closed lids, wishing so vainly that it would all be over soon.

I'd never ever imagined being trapped in the middle of a grisly bloodbath like this, but I knew it couldn't last forever. All I could do was tuck in and wait it out the best I could while hoping Dante would be all right.

Guns continued to be fired, but over the din, I heard him call for me. "Nina! *Nina!*" The desperation in his shouts saddened me.

I couldn't risk opening my mouth. I didn't want to swallow a drop of blood or brains or—

Oh, fuck. Just the thought of it had me retching. I turned, pivoting my head to the floor, and vomited.

Before I could inhale again to prime myself to heave harder, my body's involuntary demand to throw up at the nauseating thoughts and cloying smell of death in here, I was hit.

The searing pierce of a bullet cut through my shoulder, and I cried out at the agony that instantly lanced through me. "Dante!"

I didn't know if he could see me. I refused to open my eyes, keeping them closed to avoid anything dripping in them. Safer in the darkness of no sight, I whimpered and waited for him to find me in this hellhole of murder and killings.

"Nina!" He'd come to me. I felt the weight of his body as he dropped to his knees, shaking the floor. As soon as his hands touched me, urging me to roll over, I gave in to the pressure of his protecting me.

"Nina." He couldn't stop repeating my name, almost as though the more he said it, the more it would stick that I was here, that he'd found me.

"She's bleeding." Franco might have said it, but I couldn't be sure. Pain filled my shoulder. It radiated down my arm and coursed along my back. The agony was so sharp, so intense, that all I had the energy to do was lie against Dante as he urged me to uncurl from the fetal position I'd tucked myself into.

Although the ache and sharp, stinging needles of inflammation claimed all my thoughts, deep down in my heart, I relaxed. With this man, with Dante championing for me, I would be all right.

He wiped at my face, cursing as he tried to clear the blood and other slimy substances from me, but I could not surrender to the urgency to see him, to look at him and trust in my vision that he was here and all would be well again. That he'd take care of me.

It felt like a dream, but as I accepted his careful hold as he lifted me, I kept my mouth shut and swallowed down the cries that I almost uttered. It hurt to move. It hurt to be repositioned. Vaguely, with the dizziness and lightheadedness that came with the loss of blood, I registered that Dante was carrying me and taking me out of this bloody room.

"You're safe, Nina," he told me as he carried me out. "You will always be safe with me."

I know. I know I will be. It was one reason I loved him. It was a cornerstone of my trust in him. Ever since running into him that fateful night almost a month ago, I *knew* that he would do everything in his power to keep me safe and secure. Not as a fake girlfriend. Not because I was a young, clueless burden or obligation. But because he cared about me, truly. I heard it in his voice and felt it in the tremor of his touch.

I might have nodded, but I felt like I was separate from my body. Refusing to open my eyes or speak, to avoid that stuff getting in me, I couldn't let him know that I heard and agreed.

"I promise you," he said as he brought me outside. The air was clearer. Faint rain drizzled down, and the sensation of being rinsed off was cathartic.

"I promise you this, Nina..." He hurried, picking up his pace and jostling me that much more that I winced. Faster and faster, I grew sleepier, but I strained to listen, to cling to his words.

Dante hoisted me higher in his arms to match his quicker gait. "No one will ever dare to touch my wife again."

31

DANTE

Dante

Eva moved to stand next to me as we looked in the window of the hospital room that Nina was in. I held my arm out to hug my niece close, and she rested her cheek on me. "Has she woken up yet?"

I shook my head. "No, but they're not worried."

"She hit her head so hard," Eva said. "I was so worried when they took her away and I saw all the blood on the corner of the table."

Sighing deeply, I nodded.

"She pushed me down, you know."

I glanced at her.

"At the sound of gunfire, she pushed me down to safety. To protect me."

I smiled slightly. "Nina is new to our world, to this lifestyle, but she doesn't need training or experience to care. She likely acted on instinct."

"I agree," Eva said. "She's a one of a kind."

And perfect for me.

"They're not worried that she's asleep, though? For concern about a brain injury?"

"No. They've taken multiple scans and MRIs."

As soon as I found Vanessa in my room, I ran out to find Nina at the spa and make sure she was safe. Eva was already rushing from the spa, calling me and alerting Romeo and a team of soldiers that the Devil's Brothers had attacked and taken Nina. Eva was shoved aside and hit—not so badly that she needed care here at the hospital. Franco led the chase toward the MC's clubhouse. He was shot and stitched up. In a matter of minutes, it became a crusade to invade the Devil's Brothers' compound.

I arrived just as Romeo and Franco were about to storm in, and when we did, it was a goddamn bloody mess.

"They're triple-checking all the blood work, too," I told her.

It would take me a long time to get over the memory of Nina covered in blood and body matter. At first, when she didn't speak or react to my shouts, I feared the worst. That she was dead. That she was injured so badly that she couldn't move or talk. That she was shell shocked and locked within herself in a mental defense.

That wasn't the case. She simply avoided opening her mouth or eyes because she was coated with nasty bodily fluids.

I hurried her here to the hospital, and I didn't need to tell them to check for any contamination. They saw her, and they responded swiftly. After cleaning her up, they coaxed her to open her mouth. An oxygen mask went over her mouth, though, and they checked her nose and eyes for any sign of anything getting in. Nothing had. Still, they took every precaution, expediting labs to make sure nothing was in her system.

Irrigating the gunshot wound on her shoulder quickly turned into an emergency surgery. The hit had her losing too much blood. While I understood how Eva would think Nina was suffering from a brain injury, the scans showed that she had a minor concussion but nothing else.

"But shouldn't she be awake?" Eva asked.

I smiled at the concern she couldn't hide in her voice. "No. She needs the rest. Her body does. All those blood tests explained why."

Eva frowned up at me. "Huh?"

"She's pregnant." This was the first time I said the words out loud, and I felt that same overwhelming sweep of amazement as I did when the doctors showed me the results.

"She's..." Eva's mouth dropped open.

"She's pregnant. So, with the loss of blood, the doctors aren't surprised that she's so fatigued." Not to mention the mental toll this whole incident would take on her. She was kidnapped. Hit her head. Faced off with men wanting to rape her. My blood boiled at that. Her phone had been recording all the way to the hospital, and as I listened to it all, I hated that she'd feared those bikers gang raping her.

Thank fuck we got there in time.

Romeo came forward, rubbing his forehead. He had been visiting Franco while he was stitched up, and between the both of them, the cleanup was underway. Bodies had to be removed from the spa. Witnesses had to be paid off.

The MC clubhouse could deal with the dead on their own. No Constella men had fallen. Some were wounded, but no one had died on our side. We'd come in with so many, there was no way the bikers could win that fight. Many fled the compound, anyway, taking off and avoiding our shootout. Reaper, unfortunately, wasn't there. Nor was Stefan, but I hadn't counted on his being there.

"Go home. Get some rest," I told my son.

He nodded, looking so damn tired, but he paused long enough to ask Eva if she wanted a ride with him.

"Yes. I have a feeling the lovebirds will want some privacy."

Romeo rolled his eyes. Eva glanced at me, though, brows raised. I took her expression as her way of asking permission to tell Romeo what I just shared with her, and I nodded.

I turned my attention back to the window, watching the nurses finish up with checking her vitals.

I'd almost lost her, and the experience only sharpened the fact that she was my world. She'd become my world, and if I ever had to charge into the enemy's lair and shoot my way to her to rescue her, I would. Time and time again.

The Devil's Brothers were, without question, my number-one enemy. Both the bikers and the Giovannis. With his enabling Vanessa to break into my home and also in helping Nina be kidnapped, he had solidified his standing as my enemy. Now and forevermore.

I would wage war, and both the Mafia rivals and the motorcycle club would know firsthand how stupid it was to ever team up against me and try to interfere with my future.

Right now, though, my focus was on Nina. I would help her to recover. I had to break the news to her, too, about her family, and that was a delicate matter that would change who she was.

I entered the room once the nurse left, and I was pleased when Nina stirred and woke up.

"Sorry. I keep dozing off." She covered her mouth with a long yawn, and I couldn't help but smile at her.

"Don't apologize." I sat and took her hand between mine. Then I lifted it to kiss her knuckles.

"You looked like you were going to say something before I fell asleep." She peered at me as she sipped from the water in her cup.

"I was."

"Where'd Romeo go?" she asked, then furrowed her brow. "He was in my room last, right?"

"He was. We have several men being stitched up and recovering here," I explained. "Romeo's been in and out of all the rooms with the injured."

I cleared my throat, hating to break this news to her, but I wouldn't put it off. The way I saw it, starting with the bad news would only make the good news sweeter afterward.

"When Franco and I broke into the clubhouse, we found Ricky."

Her expression fell, and she lowered her gaze for a moment. "Dead?"

I squeezed her hand. "Yes." This woman had such a big heart. I knew she would be upset about her brother's death. Even though he set her up for hell and was so greedy and selfish as to bet on her life, she was a giving sort of sibling.

"I feared that would happen. When I didn't go to Reaper after the bet…"

I tipped her chin up and kissed her cheek. "You couldn't have saved him, Nina."

"I know." But she hated it, anyway.

"Ricky messed with the wrong people. He was wrong to bet on you with them. And his choices—his, not yours—caught up to him."

"I'd been thinking that even if I had gone to Reaper and fulfilled that bet, the bikers could've hurt him or killed him, anyway." A shudder ran through her, and she closed her eyes on a heavy breath. "I saw and felt just how terrible those men are."

"Were," I corrected. Because all the Devil's Brothers who'd been in that room were dead, killed by me and my men.

"With the help of your recording, we will be able to chase down and end the whole club," I told her.

"Good. Even though I hated what Ricky did to me, he was family. I'd like to know they won't just get away with that." She frowned again, studying the sheet. "Now I have no family."

"You do." I smiled slowly, glad I could follow up the news about her brother's death with the discovery of her pregnancy.

"With you?" she asked.

"Fuck yeah." I chuckled. "And Romeo and Eva. The whole Constella organization will be your family."

She started to smile, but it didn't reach her eyes.

"And our child."

She went still, staring at me. "What?" she asked on a quiet exhale.

"They've been very thorough with blood tests since you were exposed. They called it a 'biohazard' concern. All clear," I rushed to add. "But in the process of doing all that blood work, they found out that you're pregnant, too."

"Oh, Dante." Tears built on her lids, but with the wide, bright smile she couldn't hide, I knew they would be tears of joy. "Really?"

"Very, very early days," I told her, repeating what the doctor said. He worded it as though Nina wouldn't have known about her condition yet. It was that early.

"So you'll have our child as family."

"And you as…" She grinned, sniffling from her joyous reaction to the news that we would bring a baby into the world.

"Your husband."

She gazed at me with so much love shining in her eyes that I choked on all the emotions rising up within me.

"I wondered if I was hearing things when you carried me out of there. I didn't want to open my eyes or my mouth."

"Understandably," I said, kissing her knuckles again.

"But I could've sworn I heard you call me your wife." Her grin was radiant and precious. Even though we'd gone through hell to reach this moment, I wanted to memorize the beauty of her happiness forever.

"No, you weren't imagining anything. I called you my wife because that was how I viewed you. I mean it. I will be marrying you as soon as you are recovered."

She tipped her chin up in a silent request for a kiss, and I obliged. I lowered my mouth to hers and kissed her until her monitor beeped, warning of an increase in her blood pressure from my getting her excited.

Gazing down at her, I cupped her face and sighed with the satisfaction that nothing would stop us from being together. Not even ourselves. "We were idiots to ever think this attraction between us was fake."

"And the love I feel for you," she added, "will always remain true."

I kissed her again, risking the beep of that monitor. "I love you, Nina."

She sighed against my lips. "And I love you."

32

NINA

Nina

A month and a half after the night Eva took me to the spa for a girls' night, I sat back and considered how much my life had changed.

"You sure you don't want to come in?" Dante asked.

I smiled, keeping the straw between my lips. Reclining in this chaise under the shade of an umbrella, I enjoyed the humid sunshine of a late summer. "Nope."

He splashed water at me, making waves in the pool. Resting his hands on the wall, he narrowed his eyes at me. "You're tempting me to get you wet."

I let the straw slide out of my mouth as I bit my lower lip. This man. The ways he made me happy. And horny.

These pregnancy hormones were no laughing matter. We made love nonstop, it seemed. I wasn't complaining, but I didn't want to get wet right now. Not like *that*, since I was still coming down from the high of his eating me out and giving me a couple of orgasms this morning.

"I don't want to get in the pool," I clarified. My hair was still damp from the shower we shared. "The appointment is in an hour."

He nodded, shrugging as he turned to dive under the surface and commence another series of laps.

Nope. I was perfectly content right here, sipping my ice water, watching my sexy fiancé cut through the water. I never tired of seeing his chiseled body, and with the sun-kissed glow of a tan and the water clinging to his skin, he looked like something straight out of a dream.

Since the moment Dante told me that I was pregnant, I felt like I had a brand-new and meaningful purpose in life. I would be a mother soon, and I couldn't get over how wonderful that sounded.

"Hey," I said as Dante paused after a few more back-and-forth trips across the pool.

"Yeah?"

"How do you think Romeo will react to having a half-brother?"

He chuckled, running his hands over his gleaming black hair to send the water flying off. "I'm not sure. He's not upset."

But isn't it sort of weird? I was younger than the man who'd basically become my stepson. Dante and I hadn't set a date for our wedding yet. We wanted to wait until the baby was born. But we would be husband and wife, officially. The gorgeous sparkler of a ring on my finger was proof of our commitment.

Even still, I doubted Romeo would ever call me his stepmom, and I refused to look upon him as my son. The age gap just didn't make sense in that regard.

"Maybe it'll help push him out of this guilt he can't shake," Dante said as he climbed out of the pool.

I was momentarily mesmerized with the tease of his rugged body on display. Rivulets of water ran over his body, tempting me to taste them and track the liquid as it streamed down. I resisted, though, sucking on my straw and reminding myself that I didn't have to jump on him *every* chance that was presented.

"I hope so," I replied as he toweled off and walked up to where I sat.

After leaning down to kiss me, he straightened and smiled. "I'm going to shower. Then we can go to the appointment."

"I'll be here waiting." This glorious sunshine was too beautiful to pass up on.

And that was the theme of my life now. Sunshine and happiness. I had my man. I didn't have to worry about money. The Devil's Brothers were now recognized as the Constellas' enemies, and they'd never get close again.

Dante had drawn the line between his crime family and theirs. The Giovannis and MC men wouldn't get close to me, and I had faith that Dante and his soldiers wouldn't fail in that regard.

After the hell of that night, therapy had gotten me far in the journey of recovering and moving on. Both physically with my shoulder and mentally from the trauma.

I was on cloud nine, despite the Constellas' being ready to wage war on the bikers and Stefan.

Being pregnant simply put me in that disposition, to be excited for the future, not nervous about it.

I had Dante to live for. Receiving his love was a huge reason for the smile on my lips. If that wasn't enough to make me happy and optimistic, the promise of the unborn baby in my stomach was. And more than that, I had the online courses for my degree to further preoccupy me. Dante didn't only want me to be satisfied sexually. He told me that he intended to give me the world. Like Eva teased at that spa night, Dante wanted to give me anything and everything I could ask for, and that included a chance to go to college and do something altruistic and good, like focusing on early-childhood literacy.

Suffice it to say, things were looking up, and that ease of a leisurely life would continue. I knew the Constellas would fight the Giovannis and Devil's Brothers again. Dante had declared war, and he would be victorious in it. That wasn't my hero worship talking. Dante was just that formidable of a Mafia boss.

I wouldn't be included in the details. I didn't want to be, and I suspected that this pregnancy and the start of my college courses were a blessing in disguise. I'd be busy, too busy, to know about the ins and outs of this war Dante had called for.

Ignorance was bliss, but I was learning that knowledge was power in this Mafia lifestyle. I didn't intend to come to all meetings and know all the details, but as I paced myself with acclimating to this world, I knew I could rely on Dante to tell me what I needed to know to keep me safe.

Life *was* good, and that was the story I'd stick with.

"Too bad Romeo can't say the same," I mumbled as I watched the water in the pool go still again.

Dante wasn't overly worried about his son's mood. The survivor's guilt that Romeo still experienced when three men were killed months ago was no simple matter. Even I could pick up on the guy's gloominess.

He was distant and always trying to work overtime, probably to avoid having free time to think and dwell.

Which can't be healthy.

But I knew my limitations. I wasn't his stepmom. I wouldn't try to be. All I could hope to offer was my friendship.

My happiness with Dante couldn't be dimmed, and it gave me a morsel of optimism. Before I met Dante, I was stuck in a rut and thinking there was no way to change my future. Now, with him, we had a new beginning, a retake on life.

Maybe if Romeo were to meet a woman and have a chance at a new beginning...

"No. Forget about it." The last time I attempted to play matchmaker was in eighth grade, when I tried to pair up Tessa with the cute jock in our grade. It failed and flopped, mostly because he explained to us that he was gay and not interested in girls like that.

Speaking of...

I pulled my phone from my pocket and swiped to the text thread I had running with Tessa. Or more like the text thread I hoped to have with my best friend. All my messages were unanswered, and I worried that finally replacing my phone could have severed my ties with her. I still had the same number. She had to be reading the messages, but she wouldn't reply.

I chewed on my lower lip, worried that something could have happened to her.

If that damn lawyer got his way with her and made her elope...

I shook my head, refusing to think the worst. She would've told me. *Right?* My life had changed so much, so quickly, but I would never forget about my past where she was concerned. Tessa was my best friend, and we wouldn't drift apart so far that we lost contact completely.

I would never leave her in the past.

"Ready?" Dante asked as he returned.

I stood, shoving aside my worries as I went to my fiancé. He took my hand, like he always did, and together, we strolled toward his car for the first "big" appointment for the baby.

And like always, he was attentive and focused on me during the drive. His love and devotion were all I'd wished for. For so long, I'd dreamed about a man like him caring for me like this. He didn't look like a serious man married to his work and business obligations. Nor did he resemble a leader preparing to wage war on the rivals who'd threatened to tear us apart.

"Penny for your thoughts?" he asked once we parked near the doctor's office.

I brought our joined hands to my lips and pressed a kiss to his knuckles. "Just being grateful," I said.

"About what?"

"For the way we both used each other to get away from others."

I waited until we both exited the car to continue. "I ran into you, literally escaping Reaper and the bikers at the Hound and Tea. It was my motivation to agree to pretend to be your girlfriend."

He grunted a laugh. "And I proposed that fake dating thing so I could get away from Vanessa and make her stop pursuing me."

I nodded, walking alongside him to enter the doctor's building.

"We were both running from others, but it was exactly what we needed to be pushed together."

He smiled down at me and squeezed my hand. "Like it was meant to be."

"Yeah." *Now and forever.* I laid my hand over my stomach, still flat but holding our child.

Meant to be, little one.

I liked the sound of that. And I vowed to make sure our baby was always loved and cared for, not abandoned to work or other callings.

I gave my heart to Dante, and I knew he'd given me his. Together, we'd be here for this baby, and I just couldn't wait to meet him or her.

Printed in Great Britain
by Amazon